parABnormal Magazine

December 2024

Edited by H. David Blalock

parABnormal Magazine
December 2024

All rights reserved. No part of this book may be reproduced or transmitted in any form or by any means, electronic or mechanical, including photocopying or recording or by any information storage and retrieval systems, without expressed written consent of the authors and/or artists.

parABnormal Magazine is a work of fiction. Names, characters, places, and incidents are products of the authors' imaginations. Any resemblance to actual events or persons, living or dead, is entirely coincidental.

Story and illustration copyrights owned by the respective authors and artists.

Cover illustration by Brian Quinn
Cover design by Laura Givens
First Printing, December 2024
Hiraeth Publishing http://www.hiraethsffh.com/

"Permutations of The Picture of Dorian Gray" originally published in *The Hatchet: The Journal of Lizzie Borden Studies*.

Vol. VI, No. 4, Issue 24   December 2024

parABnormal Magazine is published quarterly on the 15th day of March, June, September, and December in the United States of America by Hiraeth Publishing, P.O. Box 1248, Tularosa, NM, 88352. ©2024 by Hiraeth Publishing. Nothing may be reproduced in whole or in part without written permission from the authors and artists. Any similarity between places and persons mentioned in the fiction or semi-fiction and real places or persons living or dead is coincidental. Writers and artists guidelines are available online at www.hiraethsffh.com. Guidelines are also available upon request from Hiraeth Publishing, P.O. Box 1248, Tularosa, NM, 88352, if request is accompanied by a self-addressed #10 envelope with a first-class US stamp. Editor: H David Blalock.

Contents

Stories
6	The Uninvited Guest by Josh Reynolds
22	The Lake Takes a Drink by Patrick Wright
28	Down at the Castaway by Manny Frishberg and Edd Vick
46	Prodigal by R. C. Capasso
62	The Coral Spas by Daniel Crow
78	In the Realm of Shadow by Gina Easton
93	Lakefront Property by Keith LaFountaine
104	Barry's Gate by Ann O'Mara Heyward
114	Doorways by J. S. Rogers
124	Druden Part 3 by Herika R. Raymer

Poems
21	Rusalka by Christian Dickinson
27	Many Purrs by Adele Gardner
	Blended Spirits by DJ Tyrer
42	Metamorphose: The Dark Door by Tanya Fillbrook
61	Paranormal Abyss by Denny E. Marshall
77	Phantoms by Gordon Linzner
103	Whispers and Shadows by Ivy B
	I'm New Here Myself by Matt Betts
123	Veils by Scott J. Couturier

Articles
148	Ghosts Can Exist! By Sonali Roy
153	The Most Haunted Places in Brazil by Livian Bonato
161	Permutations of *The Picture of Dorian Gray* by Denise Noe

Illustrations
123	Thorns of Life by Sonali Roy

A Little Help, Please

In the world of the small indie press we fight a never-ending battle for attention to our work, as writers and in publishing. Here's an example: big publishers [you know who they are] have gobs of $$$ that they can devote to advertising and marketing. Here at Hiraeth Publishing, our advertising budget consists of the deposits for whatever soda bottles and aluminum cans we can find alongside the highways. Anti-littering laws make our task even more difficult . . . 9

That's where YOU come in. YOU are our best promoter. YOU are the one who can tell others about us. Just send 'em to our website, tell them about our store. That's all. Just that.

Of course, we don't mind if you talk us up. We're pretty good, you know. We have some award-winning and award-nominated writers and artists, plus other voices well-deserving to be heard [not everyone wins awards, right?] but our publications are read-worthy nevertheless.

That number once again is:

www.hiraethsffh.com

Friend us on Facebook at Hiraeth Publishing

Follow us on Twitter at @HiraethPublish1

What???
No subscription to
parABnormal Magazine??

We can fix that . . .
Just go here and order:
https://www.hiraethsffh.com/product-page/parabnormal-magazine-subscription

or scan

*...also makes a great gift
any time of the year*

The Uninvited Guest
Josh Reynolds

"Well, this is dashed nuisance, what?" Charles St. Cyprian said. The cramped garret room smelled of incense, cigarette smoke, and something else. Something sweetly rancid, like spoiled meat or rotting flowers. He waved a hand in front of his face, trying to dispel the odour. "One has better things to do on a night like this."

"Does one?" Ebe Gallowglass said, as she set the heavy Gladstone bag down on the table. She pushed up the brim of her flat cap and studied the room's silent occupants warily. They sat around the hardwood table in silence, hands linked, eyes locked on sights other than the face of the person across from them. Two men and three women, all dressed to the nines, for a night out in the West End. On the table was a bolt of purple cloth, likely pinched from an inobservant vicar, a scattering of vaguely occult bric-a-brac, and a skull.

"One most certainly does, apprentice-mine." At the back of the room, Guido Gialdini whistled 'The Sheik of Araby' through the flaring horn of an old gramophone, which was perched precariously on a small stand. St. Cyprian went to it and lifted the needle, silencing Guido in mid-trill. He turned back to the table.

St. Cyprian studied the skull, careful not to touch it. It was old. Brown and cracked, with teeth missing from its jaw. There was a puckered hole in the centre of its cranium. Freshly dug up, to judge by the soil collected in the crevices. Someone had scratched various nonsensical alchemical symbols into the flaking bone, probably to make it more impressive looking.

"Assistant, innit?" Gallowglass said, opening the Gladstone. Inside, the tools of their trade—vials of dust scraped from the stones of lost pyramids, the finger-bones of forgotten saints and other, more esoteric items.

"What?"

"I'm your assistant."

"So you keep reminding me," St. Cyprian said. "Has it

ever occurred to you that they are, in fact, the same thing?" He studied the table and the silent forms occupying it. They were still alive, thankfully. Death had a tendency to complicate these matters.

Gallowglass paused, as if considering this. "Says you."

"I assure you, they are."

"Bollocks."

"Quite." St. Cyprian frowned and reached into his jacket for his cigarette case. The sickly-sweet smell was growing worse, or else he was simply becoming more aware of it. It was not a natural odour. Too pervasive for that. It was the smell of the abnatural. The stench of the Outside, seeping in. It was an aroma that he, as the current occupant of the offices of the Royal Occultist, was all too familiar with.

Founded during the reign of Elizabeth the First, the office of Royal Occultist was charged with the investigation, organization, and occasional suppression of the eldritch, infernal and unnatural, by order of the Crown. Beginning with the diligent amateur, Dr. John Dee, the office had passed through a succession of hands in its long, unwieldy history. Here and now, in the year of our Lord, 1923, those responsibilities rested with him.

Well, with him and his apprentice. By tradition, every Royal Occultist was required to take one, and Gallowglass was his, for better or worse. In time, his responsibilities would pass to Gallowglass, though neither of them was in any particular hurry to discuss the inevitable. There was still time yet, and even if there wasn't, he wasn't certain he wished to know about it. Irresponsible perhaps, but there it was.

He glanced at Gallowglass as he lit a cigarette. The two of them were a study in contrasts. He was tall, with an olive cast to his features and hair just a touch too long to be properly fashionable. His linen suit was well-tailored, straight from Gieves and Hawkes, in Savile Row. Everything about him screamed 'swell'.

Gallowglass, on the other hand, was dark and slightly feral looking, with black hair cut in a razor-edged bob and a battered flat cap resting high on her head. She wore a man's clothes, hemmed for a woman of her small stature. He knew this, because they were his clothes, stolen from his closet, and altered with money stolen from his secret biscuit tin. Gallowglass was not a believer in the concept of private property.

Given what she'd been wearing when they met, he didn't begrudge her the clothes. Charity began at home, and all that.

They'd been called to the garret by an inspector of his acquaintance, who felt that the business was outside of Scotland Yard's remit. With all due respect to the inspector, he was right. Certain things man was not meant to know, not if he wanted to sleep soundly at night. That went for plods as well as spiritualists.

"That stink is familiar," Gallowglass said. She scanned the room, eyes narrowed.

"It should be; you've smelled it often enough." He circled the table slowly, pausing once or twice to knock on the hard wood. "That, my dear Miss Gallowglass, is the smell of a bad decision." He paused beside the woman he supposed was the medium, given her suitably exotic attire, and studied her. Her countenance was hollow and wasted, her skin waxy and cool—not cold though, not yet. From a casual inspection, the others were much the same, to a greater or lesser degree. They didn't have much time.

Most of the time, séances were harmless enough. Emotionally manipulative, perhaps, but generally lacking in actual danger to the participants. But sometimes... things went wrong. Given what he saw here, this seemed to be one of those times.

The spirit world was akin to a wide, dark sea, and the waking world, a reef. Leave the reef, you risked attracting the attentions of predators. Even in the reef, you sometimes risked provoking something hungry. "Before we go any further, I need to see what we're dealing with," he said.

"That a good idea, then?" Gallowglass said, her tone making it clear that she thought it wasn't. "You could get caught up in whatever it is."

"Yes, you're right. Let's just burn the place down, shall

we?"

She shrugged. "Worked that time on Shaftsbury Avenue, remember? The slug-house? With all of the slugs?"

He grimaced. "Yes, all too well." He shook his head. "But this isn't Shaftsbury Avenue, and I don't think that this is the spectre of a primordial gastropod." He hesitated. "At least, I hope not." He waved the thought aside. "Never mind. Back in a tick."

He closed his eyes, concentrating. He reached out and traced the sacred shape of the Voorish Sign in the air as his inner eye flickered open. Some adepts called it the spirit-eye, though his acquaintances in the Society for Psychical Research insisted that it was merely a very focused form of extrasensory perception.

Whatever it was, it had taken him years to learn how to employ it safely. Humans were, by and large, as sensitive to the paranormal as animals were to earthquakes. They simply couldn't process it as well. Humans needed reasons for things which animals took on instinct. The inability of the average mind to understand all of its observations was also one of its best defences. But sometimes, you were forced to shuck the blinders first thing, otherwise you risked being snapped up unawares. As the unfortunates at the table—and Asbury—had discovered. The smell grew worse as he let his senses expand.

The room went soft, and thin, like a piece of cloth frayed to the edge of dissolution. Colors without description pulsed at the edge of his vision, and everything took on a stretched, impressionistic quality. He could make out the Ka-glow of the people seated at the table, faint, and flickering, like candles in the wind. The air was thick with icy smog and the faint echoes of Gialdini's whistling had become a train-whistle shriek.

From above the table, something turned its head to look at him.

He froze, wondering if it knew that he could see it. Then, he realized that it didn't matter. It knew he was there. And it was hungry.

It didn't have a proper shape. It was like...clay, stretched and shapeless. A splash of ectenic extrusion, rising from the skull like smoke from a chimney. The skull was the focus, then. He'd expected as much. Something inside it had been waiting for the right moment to blossom and grow, like some corrupt seed.

Feathery fronds twitched in the air, as if tasting his scent. It pulsed and shifted, forming apertures that might have been mouths and bulges that might have been eyes. It was—or had been—singing along with Gialdini, humming, vibrating its strands. Several of those fleshy barbs were wrapped about the forms of those seated at the table. The thickest was attached to the medium, which made sense—if she had awakened the spirit, it would have latched onto her first. Then the others in the circle, before any of them realized something was amiss.

Contrary to popular belief, ghosts came in all shapes and sizes. Some were less lonely spirits than they were self-aware cancers, leeching sustenance from people or places, or both. This appeared to be one such. A Saiitii manifestation, or the seed of such. A spiritual malignancy or fungus, growing stronger and more real as it battened on the Ka of its victims.

St. Cyprian frowned. "You are an ugly thing, aren't you?" His stomach roiled as the smell seemed to grow stronger and stronger, inundating him. There was no telling who it had been, if it had ever been anyone at all. Sometimes these things were just...dirt, caught between two layers of the universe.

The mass stiffened. Blister-like eyes rolled in his direction. An unattached strand undulated languidly towards him. He took his cigarette from his mouth and jabbed the lamprey like protuberance, causing it to retreat. The cigarettes were hand-rolled by an acquaintance in Limehouse—a special Moro blend, offensive to certain spirits. He stepped back and allowed his spirit-eye to shut, restoring the world to reassuring solidity.

"That you?" Gallowglass asked warily. Her fingers inched into her coat, towards the shoulder holster holding the Webley-Fosbery revolver she habitually kept close to hand. Sometimes things tried to hitch a ride back, if you stayed in the dark for too long.

"'s me, innit?" he said, mimicking her. He took a long drag and blew a plume of smoke in her direction. The cigarette helped to calm him. The ol' nerves got a bit jangly, on occasion, after seeing the horrors that lay beneath.

"Go chase yourself." Then, "What'd you see?"

"Nothing pleasant." He stepped back from the table. "We'll need to break the connection, first and foremost. See if we can jolt whatever it is into retreating. And maybe get some answers as to what this was all about in the process." Pulling the participants apart was usually the simplest way, and the best. He gestured towards one of the men. A big chap, full soup and fish, with a Clark Gable moustache on a bulldog face. "We'll start with him. He looks fairly doughty, in an unfashionable sort of way. It probably hasn't been feeding on him as long."

"We don't even know what *it* is yet," Gallowglass said.

He rubbed his hands together. "Thrill of discovery, Miss Gallowglass. Now, help me yank him out of his chair."

"Sure that's smart?"

"Only one way to find out. Grab his shoulder."

Luckily, the grips of the other participants on their chosen test-subject were loose. He came free of the circle with a wet thump. St. Cyprian looked down and then up, at Gallowglass. "I thought you were going to catch him."

"Your idea, innit?"

The man groaned. St. Cyprian pulled a vial of smelling salts out of his pocket and sank to his haunches. He waved the salts under the man's nose and helped him to sit up. "Up we go, there's a good chap."

"W—what?"

"Trade the ol' horizontal for the vertical, what?" The smell had changed, subtly, and for the worse. He looked at Gallowglass, who nodded, her eyes narrowed. She could feel it as well, whatever it was. A definite worsening of the general atmosphere. Their trick had only agitated it, rather than forcing a retreat, as he'd hoped.

The man stared at him, blinking. "What?"

"Exactly. Who are you, then?"

"A—Asbury. Paul Asbury. Of the Sussex Asburys." Asbury looked around. He shivered, and clutched at himself, as if he were cold. "What's going on? Who are you? What happened?"

"Rather hoping you could answer that, old man," St. Cyprian said, as he helped Asbury to stand. Asbury shoved him aside brusquely.

"I don't need help," he growled, despite the obvious weakness of his limbs.

"Pull the other one," Gallowglass said. Asbury glared at her.

"Who are you people?"

"A better question is, what was this all about?" St. Cyprian said. He peered at Asbury. There was a distinct familial resemblance among the participants at the table. All of them were of a similar age. Siblings then, or cousins. He decided to risk the latter. "Why were you and your...cousins partaking in this excursion to the demimonde?"

"I don't see where it's any of your business, whoever you are," Asbury said. His hands knotted into fists. He had the look of a man who didn't like being asked questions.

"Oh, there you are quite mistaken," St. Cyprian said. He reached into his coat for his cigarette case. His hand froze as Guido Gialdini began to whistle again. St. Cyprian glanced at the gramophone, and then at Gallowglass, who shrugged. Asbury made to speak, but St. Cyprian silenced him with a gesture. "I think we woke it up," he said.

"Woke what up?" Asbury said. "What the devil is going on?"

"Quiet," St. Cyprian said. The air felt wet and close. It was getting hard to breathe.

He reached into his coat pocket, feeling through the various amulets and charms which he carried with him at all times. One never knew when one might need an Assyrian demon-whistle, or a silver coin blessed by Prester

John. Neither of those was what he was looking for, however.

He extracted a tiny copper vial, engraved with Arabic characters, stoppered with wax. He flicked his thumbnail across the wax and opened the vial, releasing a small amount of powder into his palm. He flung the powder out about him, and the air took on a shimmery haze reminiscent of the open desert at midday. A looping, lamprey tendril bled into view, as the powder did its work.

"Bleedin' Nora," Gallowglass cursed, reaching for her pistol.

St. Cyprian waved her back. "Chalk," he said. "And quickly. You know what to do." He puffed on his cigarette, filling the immediate area with smoke. The tendril retreated. He knew he'd only bought them a few moments, at most.

Gallowglass rummaged in the Gladstone and found the chalk. It had been made from the powdered bones of saints. Which ones, he wasn't exactly sure, but it seemed to do the trick. Swiftly, she bent and began to draw a wide pentacle on the wooden floor. As she worked, St. Cyprian retrieved something else from the bag—a tightly wrapped bundle, held shut by brass buckles.

'What—what is that thing?" Asbury said, staring in stupefaction at the twisting, eel-like extrusion. It had come no closer, but St. Cyprian knew it was only a matter of time before it gained the strength to do so. Soon, it would suck its captives dry, and seek out new prey. It would go after Asbury first, and then he and Gallowglass, with all the desperate hunger of a famine victim. He began to unbuckle the bundle.

"A ghost."

"A ghost?"

The way Asbury said it caused St. Cyprian to pause. "Yes. It's feeding off of your cousins, and the medium. As it was feeding off of you, until we pulled you loose."

"My cousins, are they—" Asbury began. He seemed enthused by the prospect.

"Not quite. Not yet. It's a bit like...a spider's web. They're all wrapped up in ectenic discharge, until it—he—

finishes the meal."

"He?"

"Well, it's a man's skull." St. Cyprian peered at him. "Out of curiosity, why were you holding a séance around a man's skull? And don't tell me it's none of my concern, because I think you've grasped by now that it jolly well is. Speak, and swiftly."

Asbury hesitated. St. Cyprian snapped his fingers impatiently. "Treasure," Asbury said, flatly, still watching the squirming tendril. "An ancestor of ours—Lord bloody Gideon bloody Asbury—was supposed to have hidden his wealth somewhere before the Parliamentarians got to him and stretched his neck."

"And you needed the money."

Asbury frowned. "An inheritance divided four ways is no sort of inheritance. The treasure would compensate for things, somewhat." His frown deepened. "Some of us had debts, if you must know."

"By which you mean you," St. Cyprian said.

Asbury grimaced. "A man has a right to enjoy himself." He cast a glare at the medium. "That witch said she could find it for a fair price. I got the others to agree, on the condition that we split it. All she had to do was ask his spirit."

"Which she needed his skull for," St. Cyprian said. "And you procured it for her, I gather?" Something billowed in a far corner. Like smoke, only...not. Smoke didn't move like that. It spread like a thing aware.

"I—yes, I did," Asbury said, sourly.

"Hanged, you said?" More not-smoke, spilling upwards from between the floorboards. It stretched, rising to almost human height. Awake, now and aware, the ghost—the entity—was beginning to influence its surroundings. Testing its boundaries.

"He was. I don't see how that matters..."

"It matters, because there's a bullet hole in that fellow's cranium."

Asbury shrugged. "Maybe the legend was wrong."

"Or maybe you got the wrong skull," St. Cyprian said. But even as he said it, he wondered if Asbury had. He wouldn't have been the first man to try and use sorcery to procure ill-gotten gains. Before he could press the point, Guido's trilling began to repeat and skip, as if something had nudged the needle. He was tempted to scatter more powder, but had little desire to see any more than he already had, until it was absolutely necessary.

"That skull has been in the family vault for decades!" Asbury blustered.

"Then someone else got the wrong skull. Either way, we are left with something of a conundrum. Because your uninvited guest isn't going to drift back off to sleep any time soon." His hackles prickled, and he looked around. The air had gone cold. His breath plumed, uncoiled, and spread, joining with that of Asbury and Gallowglass. No more time for mysteries, then. "Finished with that circle yet, Miss Gallowglass?"

"Do you want to do this?" she said, still on the floor.

"No, no, but haste would be appreciated." He studied the vague, thin, shapes as they drifted. There were more of them now, and the smell from before was almost unbearable. They weren't quite human shaped, nor did they resemble the formless tendrils he'd seen. He glanced at the skull, wondering who it had been, and where Asbury had really found it. Saiitii manifestations didn't form spontaneously. They required mental and spiritual trauma of the most diabolical sort to inculcate the focus. "Give it some welly, if you would."

Gallowglass responded with a vulgar euphemism, eliciting a startled cough from Asbury. St. Cyprian chuckled and finished unbuckling the bundle. He cast the cloth aside to reveal a long dagger of unique design. It was a heavy thing, with a wedge shaped blade, and a thin hilt squeezed between an ornate crosspiece and a heavy pommel. The blade was etched with strange sigils, and devilish faces, with wicked tusks and protruding tongues, had been carved upon the crosspiece.

"What the deuced sort of heathen pokery is that?" Asbury asked, staring at it in disgust. "I've never seen the like."

"I expect not." St. Cyprian extended the blade and

sighted down the length. The indistinct shapes were almost visible in the frost-tinged air. More lamprey-tendrils, perhaps, but visible now, as the manifestation stirred to full wakefulness. The séance had woken it, and his observations had caught its attention. He could feel the full weight of its malignant awareness, pressing down on him from all directions. A quaquaversal imposition, fumbling at his senses. He slashed out, and felt a quiver on the air.

"This blade was crafted before Hyperborea was buried in ice, and forged by a puissant sorcerer of that time, who made the hilt from the fang of an immense worm," he said. "The sigils are Lemurian, the iron, Atlantean, and the scabbard, Elizabethan." He slashed again, around the edges of the circle. "The latter was made from dried and cured skin stripped from the back of a Basque magician who tried to wreak a terrible working on Queen Elizabeth." A third time, and a third quiver on the air. A vibration, as if of sudden retreat. "The fire that was used in its forging was kindled by a salamander, and dead men worked the bellows."

"None of that actually answers my question, dash it!"

"It's a knife, formerly belonging to one John Subtle, an alchemist of uncertain disposition," St. Cyprian said, with a sigh. No one appreciated a good pedigree anymore. "It cuts through spirit-matter as if it were flesh."

"A bloody knife isn't going to do any good against— against *that*," Asbury snarled, pointing at the indistinct shapes now gathering about them. "We need to run..."

"And leave your siblings behind?"

"Well I'm certainly not carrying them out." Asbury started for the door.

"I wouldn't," St. Cyprian said. "The ghost..."

Asbury gestured sharply and crudely. St. Cyprian blinked. Gallowglass laughed. "Guess he told you. Circle's finished, by the way."

St. Cyprian tightened his grip on the knife. "Asbury— come back to the circle. *Now.*"

Asbury had almost made it to the door when the shapes stiffened. Abruptly, St. Cyprian realized his mistake. They weren't figures, or even tendrils. They were *fingers*. Fingers that snapped shut about Asbury's bulky form with inhuman quickness. Asbury screamed as the pale things closed about him with sudden, bone-crunching force. St. Cyprian cursed and lunged. The ghost-knife sang out and passed through a pale knuckle. The fingers sprang open, and a sound like thunder shook the garret room. Asbury collapsed against St. Cyprian, wheezing.

"Oi, watch it," Gallowglass called out. He turned, saw more fingers descending from the ceiling. Like a man reaching into a matchbox. He slashed out with the knife, and the fingers retreated, wriggling. He half-dragged the shuddering Asbury into the circle and dropped him to the floor. The man fell with a groan. He likely had a few broken bones, but that was better than the alternative.

"Oh Lord, it's bloody killed me," he groaned.

"You're not dead yet," St. Cyprian said. "Though, now might be a good time to unburden the old conscience, what?"

"What do you mean?"

"The skull—it's not the one you were sent for, was it?"

Asbury's eyes widened, and St. Cyprian knew his guess had been correct. "Whose skull did you bring, Asbury?"

"I don't know, damn you," Asbury said, clutching at his chest. "The medium—that witch—she swore she could find the treasure, but I—I..."

"Didn't want to share it," Gallowglass said, matter-of-factly. "Pulled a switch. Come back later with the real one, innit?" She tapped the side of her head. "Cunning, like."

Asbury glared at her, his face beginning to swell with bruises. "I needed the money."

"And your greed may have doomed us all. Jolly well done." St. Cyprian patted him companionably on the shoulder, eliciting another groan from the injured man. The giant fingers probed about the edge of the circle in a questing fashion.

Gallowglass had one hand on her revolver. "More than ten of them, innit?" she said, after a moment. The fingers scratched at the air about the circle like curious cats. They wouldn't be able to pierce the circle. But it wouldn't hold them back forever.

St. Cyprian looked at her. "That's what bothers you about this?"

She shrugged. "Just an observation. What's the plan?"

"This situation calls for a bit of ectenic surgery, I believe. The sooner, the better, if our friend here was telling the truth." God alone knew what Asbury had brought to the party. He'd have to find out where Asbury had gotten the skull, but later. If there was a later. Thinking quickly, he said, "We'll break the connections one by one. When it's weakened a bit, I daresay it'll retreat. And once it does..."

She cocked her revolver. "Simple, innit?"

"Yes, well, wait until I'm out of the way, please." He reached into his pocket and found the vial of powder. He tossed it to her. "Throw it over the skull and shoot. Keep its attention, if you can."

She gave a lazy salute. "Try not to get eaten, if you can."

"I wouldn't give you the satisfaction," he said. He took a breath, and stepped out of the circle. The fingers dipped towards him, smacking together in hideous fashion. He swept the ghost-knife out, cutting through their milky substance. The fingers retracted, and he felt, rather than heard, a moan of protest. It reminded him of an animal being refused food. The Asbury cousins twitched in their seats, as if whatever held them was quivering in rage. He reached the table and said, "Miss Gallowglass, if you please."

Behind him, he heard the crack of Gallowglass' Webley. A rain of dust fell across the table, revealing the squirming tendrils he'd seen earlier. Swiftly, he chopped through the closest one, freeing one of the cousins. He upended her chair unceremoniously and sent her toppling backwards, away from the table. A sub-dermal groan echoed through his bones as another connection was broken, and he shot a glance towards the skull.

The thing rising from it was taking on a firmer shape.

It might have been a face, albeit one moulded by a child or a lunatic, and stretched to impossible size. It silently gnashed tombstone teeth in an idiot's leer. He'd seen worse, but not lately. The sight of it paralyzed him, for just an instant, but long enough to almost cost him dearly. It reached for him again, plucking at his legs and neck. He fell back against the table, chopping at the semi-solid digits. Out of the corner of his eye, he saw Gallowglass lunge forward and grab the back of another cousin's chair. She yanked it back, severing the connection, and spilling the unconscious man to the floor.

The bulging eyes of the spirit revolved slowly, seeking this new disruption. It was still uncertain, unfocused. That was their only advantage. St. Cyprian took the opportunity to break away from its groping fingers and lunge for a third cousin. The ghost-knife sang down, gouging the table. The floorboards rattled beneath his feet and Gialdini's whistle had risen to a screech of frustration. That left only one—the medium. The ghost-knife was warm in his hand, and pellucid matter clung to the blade. "Be ready to move," he shouted, as he hacked away at a questing finger.

The abominable face rippled towards him, jaws wide. It was speaking, a low rumble of sound rising beneath the whistling on the gramophone. His skull ached from the force of it, and he stumbled. It was like being caught in a turbine. He sucked the last erg of heat from his cigarette and expelled the smoke into its mad, yellow eyes.

It blinked, and the pressure eased. St. Cyprian caught hold of the medium. She thrashed in his grip, like a drowning woman. He thrust the knife home, piercing the tendril that snared her throat. It reared back, glistening stick-pin teeth oscillating in a narrow mouth. The tendril lunged for him, and he chopped through it.

Fingers thumped into him like clubs, and he gasped in pain. A monstrous hand climbed up his legs like a spider, squeezing his middle. Another reached down, as if to twist his head off. The spirit was still speaking, and he caught a ragged pulse of what might have been antiquated English —nonsense syllables, but recognizable for all that. Its yellow orbs bulged like straining balloons in its stretched features, inhuman and incomprehensible.

Desperate now, he sent the medium toppling to the floor with a convulsive heave as he was whipped off of his feet and hurled into the gramophone. It fell silent with a squawk, and he rolled aside as fingers snapped down, cracking floorboards. The substance of the hand wavered and faded, reduced to drifting motes.

Adrenaline and fear lending him speed, St. Cyprian backed towards the table. With no physical tethers, the spirit was anchored solely to the skull. It twisted like an animal, lunging wildly against the bars of some invisible cage, but dwindling as it did so. Without a source of nourishment, it was shrinking away, tumbling back into somnolence. He sliced away at any questing tendrils, keeping it at bay. Behind him, Gallowglass dragged a cursing, protesting Asbury from the circle. "Ready when you are," she said, over his groans of pain.

In a matter of moments, the great face had crumpled into a toddler's grimace, and then into the barest memory of a visage. The skull resembled an anemone, covered in twisting, tubular fingers, clutching at nothing.

St. Cyprian slid the point of the ghost-knife through an eye-socket and lifted the skull from the table. Carefully, hands shaking, he carried it to the circle, and tossed it inside. The smoky excess faded fully, retracting into the shadowed recesses of the skull. Something that might have been an eye glared out of the bullet hole in the cranium.

"Now what?" Gallowglass asked, staring down at the skull.

"Now, we wait. It'll settle down eventually, and we can properly contain it, or exorcise it, as the situation warrants." He pulled out his cigarette case, and selected a new one before offering it to Gallowglass.

"And then?" she asked, taking one.

"Add it to the collection, I suppose," he said. He struck a match and lit her cigarette. "It'll look dashed swell on the mantle, don't you think?"

Rusalka
Christian Dickinson

The young man gazed upon the silent stream
Of dark Danube upon a summer's night,
When from the depths, a form of fair delight
Enrobed in mists arose as from a dream.

The fair-skinned beauty leant upon the youth:
"My love," she said, "lie down with me a space,
And let us pass our time in love's embrace.
We'll take our pleasure—banish pain and ruth."

The youth demurred, "My love lives in the town,
And I to her have pledged my constant troth."
The fair maid's eyes changed to a jealous green.
Her robes dispersed, and gold hair lost its sheen.
Her lovely form turned ugly, old, and wroth,
And drew the youth beneath the water's crown.

The Lake Takes a Drink
Patrick Wright

My first thought, of course, was *How did he end up there?* It was a man standing on a rock out in the lake, out in a rural part you can't see from the beach or the boat ramp, near enough to shore but beyond wading distance. The man was wearing your quintessential fisherman's garb. A bucket hat and a vest of pouches. Dressed not too terribly unlike myself.

He was smiling softly and waving, ratcheting an upraised hand back and forth in friendly mechanical greeting, and he wasn't wearing any shoes. He wasn't wet, either. There was no boat nearby, nothing he could've leapt onto the rock from that could've then floated away.

But none of that gave me pause. Strange things happen all the time. Who knows what confederation of bizarre happenstances could've ordered themselves up in a line that wound up at the dry man waving at me from that rock. No, that wasn't what gave me pause.

What gave me pause were his feet. They were all wrong. They clung to the rock, folded around it. Like there weren't bones in them, or weren't bones in the proper places. I felt a weird tingle in my temple like the onset of a migraine and kept motoring my little flat bottom boat right along past the man, watching him but ignoring his gentle beckoning.

I kept looking back at him till I rounded a bend in the lakeshore and he disappeared behind the pine trees. He was turned around watching me go, though something said it was only for my benefit, a way to keep up the act, and that he didn't need to turn at all to see where I was.

It wasn't until dinner that night back at the cabin that I started getting the sweats thinking, *What did he want from me? If he was no man, which he wasn't, why was he waving at me? Why would he beckon me over? What could he have possibly had in mind for me?* I kept eating my dinner and scraped the bowl loud enough to shut my mind up.

It was such an insane and absurd thing I thought - *this thing is no man* - that it wasn't too far into the evening hours before I started second guessing myself. The mind is an easy thing to trick and that goes both ways. You can fixate on a thing and make it true, make yourself certain that that girl at the diner really *does* like you or that those two guys at the bait shop really *are* always laughing at you when you come in. The same can also be said for making true things untrue, especially odd things like falsified totem pole men perched on rocks like resting birds, men carved out of lake matter and molded of mud. It is a tough thing to admit to yourself you believe, let alone to let on to others. Much easier to accuse yourself of hysteria and move on.

Because I didn't really see a monster man with misshapen feet clinging to a rock out on the lake. I saw an embarrassed fellow in a great deal of trouble who couldn't swim terribly well who needed a ride back to shore. He was a hitchhiker on the lake tide. And I had left him there to suffer who knows what when I abandoned him out there. I wondered what my wife would think if I told her after getting back from the lake trip what a coward I'd been and for what little cause. He could've slipped off, could've drowned, could've seen me staring at him till I rounded the trees to leave and thought, *Man, the nerve of some people. There goes my faith in the human condition.*

That one was what really did me in and decided me to go back and check in on the fellow, hoping that I wouldn't get there and find some cartoon evidence of his drowning, his bucket hat left behind floating on the water lapping at the lakeshore on licking waves like a dog tongue tickling its dish rim for scraps. Like a hungry man sucking the brains out of shrimp heads.

I shuddered to think.

I knew better than that. I knew that despite glassy serene appearances the lake had a hot darkness simmering in its belly. I knew folks had a habit of taking to the lake and the lake a habit of taking them with it, ushering them underneath it to show them the way the lake weeds danced at the bottom with the fish weaving between them. It was such a show no one ever came up again. It wasn't infrequent that tourists and day trippers would travel to our lake on a holy tour of summer lands with such sights to see and only be missed when their spouses came calling their names on the beaches and in the bait shops. We would just say, *There's another one gone.* I was out here often enough - most weekends, sometimes with the lady and our kids - that the bait shop boys considered me a townie and we spoke of it. We would say, *Usually we drink from the lake. Every so often, the lake wants a drink from us.*

So I set out in the early morning hours to seek recompense. I was shaking my head the whole way, damning myself for considering whatever it was that had gone running its circles round this fool head of mine. What was my wife going to think?

It was early, so nobody was out, and I had pretty much the whole lake to myself. It was quiet and still and showed me back the sky reflected across its wide upraised belly like a trickster making monkey shines. Trying to disorient me and confuse me. You can't fall into the sky, but you can fall into the lake. If you get them turned around enough, they won't know which way is up and they'll have to start making guesses. That's when you've got them, the lake says. That's when the hook sets.

My motor rumbled its feeble little hum across the surface until the trees along the shoreline muffled the noise at the lake edges. I came back around to the rural end of the water, where there are fewer houses than where our vacation home lies and where there are many nooks and crannies to swing in and out of in search of the fish occupying the deep and obscure spots. Those are the good fish; the ones no one's found yet. That's why it takes skill to do a fisherman's duty.

I thought for a hopeful moment that I wouldn't be able to find the same little inlet again. One corner of the lake looks the same as the other, and this lake has many corners.

But I spotted the hat quickly enough. It wasn't terribly far from the rock I had seen the man perched upon, but it was no longer occupied. At least not as much as I could tell. It was set upright on the water like the lake itself was wearing it, but I suppose just about anyone could've been crowned by that hat hidden beneath the shimmering glass of the stillwater, which still wouldn't give up what it held underneath so much as reflect your own features back at you like how some fish will spit in your face when they come to the surface.

And my heart sank at the sight of it, and I went to lamenting, "Oh lord, oh lord."

I stood up and looked down on it with my hands on my hips, wondering just how it was gonna affect the rest of my days living with a thing like this. With it in the back of my head. Would I even tell my wife now? Sometimes the shame is too much on things. I never told her when I fell and busted my ass on the porch back home when it iced up last winter for much the same reason.

I had cut the engine and let myself drift along, but the momentum kept carrying me forward toward the hat nonetheless, like guiding me toward it. It was my sin after all, might as well make good and sure I knew it belonged to me. It was drawing me closer like pulling in a line, reeling me in lithely one hand reaching in and smoothly tugging back, then the other.

With a bit of effort I positioned myself on my aching knees on the bottom of the boat, leaned forward and reached for the hat. I looked down at the lake surface. It was when it gave up its reflection for me, let the curtain drop and let me see down into its recesses, that I recognized my error. But it was too late; I was hanging halfway out of the boat, halfway over the water, and the hat was almost within reach. And it's an absurd thing to admit to a thing like that. To just *knowing*. So you'll cast it aside, you'll reject it. There's no inhuman thing on that rock, and there's no sunken man in the lake. That's just silly.

But as confirmation, I saw him coming. He was coming quickly, had practiced this most assuredly. It's like any good fisherman; you've got to set the hook quick and clean, and reel them in fast. It takes skill to do a fisherman's duty.

He hadn't retained his shape overnight. I suppose it takes a great deal of effort to keep it up like that, even for the simple likes of me. It wasn't just his feet that were wrong now, but the whole swirling length of him. There wasn't much head to put a hat back on, now. Or else there was too much. It was hard to tell what was lake shimmer and what was manflesh. It was like tensing a muscle, and keeping it contracted in the shape of a fellow, how that would look once you've finally let go of your grip.

Oh yes, I realized in some distant way as he pulled me in, *he is a hitchhiker on the lake tide. Yes he is indeed; he is no man, but he is a hitchhiker, and he wants to hitch a ride out of this lake.* I suppose they all do. The last thought that ran through me as I was ushered down deep by the soft rushing hand of the waterman to join the rest of its hoarded collection of rusted goodies at the lake bottom was *what will my wife think?* and then I saw it clear as day: I saw her wandering the lakeshore, wandering the beaches and into the bait shops, calling my name. A lost name on a missing poster. There's another one gone.

But then, what's to stop her from seeing me on the beach, coming up from the water sopping wet, because a hook finally set somehow in me unlike in so many of those others, and I'll be smiling apologetically and waving, and I am no longer myself, but instead a lakefaring daytripper on a visit inland? What sights he'll have to see.

Oh, it's bound to happen sooner or later. The lake has been trying long enough.

Many Purrs
Adele Gardner

What a lovely life we have together:
me and all my cats, the living and the dead,
the ghosts of their little paws joining me in the night,
alongside their warm, purring brothers,
drawn to our love like fire.
"We'll never let you disappear, don't worry.
Don't worry," I promise them,
and they purr in reassurance,
We're still here.

Blended Spirits
DJ Tyrer

There's a bar somewhere in New York City
A dingy basement affair, uninviting
That serves the strangest of spirits
I don't mean alcohol, no
Nor do I mean the customers are ghosts
Although the drinks are…
They take two or more souls from bottles
Blend and shake them into one
And serve them with a slice of lemon
To their select clientele
And, the drinks are cheap for those willing
Or, daring… promising their souls upon death
To be collected in a bottle
One day to be blended in a drink…

Down at the Castaway
Manny Frishberg and Edd Vick

Casey Ryan drained the last of her vodka-7 and set the glass on its napkin, watching a lone ice cube settle, then looked up into Dana Palace's eyes. They were soft, expressive and anticipatory. Casey stared into those large green eyes and weighed her next move. They were enticing and made her chest tingle with excitement. But that only reminded her that she wished it were Andie making her feel light-headed and desired.

Casey decided, pulling a legal-size envelope from her purse onto her lap. "No," she said when Dana stirred, ready to be out the door with her. "You're being served."

After a moment of amused disbelief, Dana narrowed her eyes. "Seriously?"

"Your husband is filing for divorce." Casey pushed the envelope over a puddle of something between their glasses until it touched Dana's hand.

Dana stared at the envelope sitting like an accusation between them. "Why did you wait until we were on a date?"

A fair question – she'd asked herself the same thing during dinner and still didn't have a good enough answer. Casey had located Dana through her SapphOnline profile, which seemed to make her fair game – she was still married, after all.

"When I called I meant to serve you right away, but then I got to your place and you looked so lonely."

Casey turned toward The Castaway's swinging doors at a noise behind her, cop instincts still operating after two years off the force. When she turned back Dana was already in motion. Casey ducked and the heavy stein sailed over her head. It rebounded off the high seat and banged into the back of her head.

Dana grabbed her purse, yelled "Asshole!" A trickle of beer slid down Casey's back. She rubbed the back of her head, then looked at her fingers. No blood, just beer. "Damn it," she said.

Dana strode to the back of the bar, disappearing through the door to the bathrooms, leaving the envelope on the table. She'd been served, technically.

Burt, the bartender, kneeled down to retrieve the missile. The thick white stein gripped in his gargantuan right hand reminded Casey of a piano keyboard. "Not even cracked," he said, his voice sounded like a bag of gravel in a tunnel. "They don't make them like that anymore. How's your head?"

"It's not cracked either, thanks for asking." She smiled wanly. "Hell, I've had worse." She'd caused worse too.

He looked toward the rear of the bar. "That was an asshole move," he said mildly. "Serving her on a date, I mean."

"She's the one going on lesbian dating sites." Casey pulled out her notebook and checked off the service, glancing at her phone to add the time. "Ideally I'd get her to sign for those papers, but I get the feeling she's not in a giving mood."

"Maybe you can catch her on the way out," said Burt, bringing her drink. "There's no back door."

A replica Fifties-style Wurlitzer jukebox stood at the end of the bar, colors shifting in glass columns filled with bubbling liquid. As a nod to the 21st century, it took bills, credit cards, or Paypal. "Sound of Sunshine," a Michael Franti and Spearhead song that was never released outside of Italy, let alone on vinyl, finished playing. Burt pulled over a chair from a nearby table.

"Pretty quiet today." There was no way he'd have fit into the narrow booth.

"Pretty quiet every day," Casey said, pulling on her soda. "It's one of the best qualities of the place."

"I could stand a little less ambiance," Burt grumbled.

"I bet." Neither one of them was much for conversation, she thought, and sipped her drink. Still, it was better than going home and talking to her cats.

The Castaway Lounge was Burt's retirement plan. He'd purchased it in the wake of the Oh-Eight recession. His timing had been right. A wave of yuppie professionals moving into the Pearl District had found the Castaway.

But he'd put everything he'd saved into it over the years and Yuppies had turned out to be an unstable commodity.

"Case, do you have time to look into something for me?"

"For you, Burt? Nothing but." She kept one eye on the door in the back.

"Before we go any further, you're gonna think it's too piddling, but I'm paying full freight for this one." Burt said, eyes down. "Somebody's been screwing around downstairs. Nothing's been taken. It's just little things -- stuff keeps getting moved around. Floors scraped and dust smeared – somebody farting around but I don't know how they manage to get past me."

"Well, I can look around, put up a few cameras. See what pops. Sound okay to you, Burt?"

"Yeah, thanks, doll," he said, smiling a little. "I never liked it down there," he went on. "Always gives me the shivers. I keep my supplies right close to the stairs and I go beyond that as little as I can."

Casey only half heard what he was saying. Only Burt called her "doll". No one else would dare call her that. Andie had dared, though, and Casey'd let her. That still meant only Burt got to use the nickname, because she could not bear having a coke-head in her life. She had demons enough of her own to worry about. Losing her partner Tom had sent her on a bender that lasted for three years and in the end cost her her shield.

"Case, did you even hear me? I asked when you could get those cameras up."

"Sorry," she said, "Old wounds. I'll get on it this evening."

Casey stood, wanting to hit the bathroom before heading to the lawyer's office. She might even "run into" Dana while she was at it, buttonhole her in a stall and get her to take the divorce papers. She went into the anteroom and stiff-armed the door painted with the picture of a life-preserver, a remnant of The Castaway's brush with hipsterdom. The room was too small for someone to hide or be missed. Maybe Dana'd picked the door with the palm tree instead. Newcomers made that mistake all the time.

She finished, then checked the men's room. It was larger but dingier, with an odor of sweat and fermenting urine under the floral air freshener. Male scents made the hair on her arms stand up, always had. The bathroom windows had long ago been painted shut. Also empty.

Casey glanced at the bar's basement door. The padlock was open but hanging on its hasp holding the door closed. If Dana had gone that way, someone had to have closed the door behind her, and no one had gone in or out. There was no way Dana could have snuck past; Casey's instincts were too sharp. It was like she'd fallen through the floor.

No matter. If she was gone, she was gone. Casey would swear an affidavit to attest she'd served the papers legally.

"I'm going to go grab those cameras," she told Burt. Casey stepped out into the glare of a Portland summer afternoon and walked over to Union Station to catch the Maxx.

At home, Casey started digging through the City website to unearth the building's history. It had started as a general store serving local businesses and ferrymen's needs in the early days. By the 1890s, when the Yukon gold rush filled the streets of every port city north of Monterey, it had become a fashionable drinking establishment, with a mahogany bar brought around the horn. Upstairs, a couple of dozen "seamstresses" rented rooms by the hour; down below, the infamous "Shanghai tunnels," where hapless sailors were hauled to the docks. She made a mental note to check the basement for access to the tunnels.

It wasn't the last time this bar had been its clientele's last stop on their way to Shanghai. Lately, along with the old timers, the bar's customers consisted mainly of young bilingual Chinese professionals, too many of whom were becoming "sea turtles," flocking back to China for higher pay.

***

About half the tables in the bar were occupied when Casey returned with her equipment stuffed into a gym bag. Instead of settling in her preferred corner booth Casey headed straight for the bar. Nora handed her a vodka and Seven-Up in a highball glass. The evening bar maid always got it right. Casey went to the cash register to pick up the key Burt had left for her. She stopped to take a long pull in her drink, set it on the bar, and walked toward the back.

A stale, musty odor greeted her when she opened the basement door. Feeling for a light switch, she found an old-fashioned Bakelite knob. Thick cloth-wrapped wires led along the ceiling joists, attached to nothing. A clip-on LED light plugged in near the stairs cast stark, heavy shadows on the stairway and the cases of wine, beer, and spirits stacked around the bottom step. She made her way down steep, narrow treads and around the boxes. The ceiling was low enough she had to stoop, so she was oppressively aware of its nearness. The back end of the storeroom barely caught the spillover light from near the stairs.

Casey tapped on her phone's flashlight app. She noticed the disturbance Burt had mentioned. It looked like some boxes had been shifted around on the floor into different configurations. Shining her light farther in, she found the thick dust lay undisturbed, and no sign of footprints. It seemed highly unlikely anyone had been here in years.

Small wonder coming down here gave Burt the creeps. The air felt thick, difficult to stir into motion, even colder than she'd have expected. The walls were brick, as befitted a building over a hundred years old. They differed in color from one part of a wall to another, likely earlier sections that had been replaced with newer brick. In some sections, the brick was covered with a coat of cement.

Walking the perimeter of the room, she examined the walls. Anyone coming down from the bar would have had to unlock the padlock and replace it when they were done, all without being noticed by anybody in the bar. Casey recalled the lore of how, during Prohibition, Old Town speakeasies had gotten their liquor through the old Shanghai tunnels.

In the very back of the cellar, there was a low circular brick arch that she could see led to a passageway. But half of the arch was filled with old pieces of broken furniture, wooden packing crates, and an ancient zinc bathtub. If Dana had tried climbing through, the dusty jumble would have been disturbed. She peered down the tunnel, but the light behind her barely reached beyond the opening.

She considered the possibility of Dana making her way out to the riverfront through the tunnels. *Not if it meant breaking a nail*, she thought. *Besides, how would she have gotten the padlock back on the hasp behind her?* Then there was there was still the matter of the lack of footprints in that area of the basement.

She found spaces where her minicams would nestle, one infrared camera and two equipped with powerful lights, crossing each other's line of view. She set them to motion-activated mode. Upstairs, in her corner booth, she fired up a cheap tablet she kept for the purpose and brought the webcams up on the screen. She set the software to record automatically when the cameras detected movement.

Most of the ice in Casey's drink had melted. She questioned Nora briefly, learning that she and the bar's dishwasher Ephraim never went to the basement. "Nobody goes down there but the boss," she said. "It's hella spooky." Before she left, Casey gave the tablet to Nora, along with the key, to stash behind the bar.

The next day, Casey served two summonses, one to a man in the middle of a root canal. During lunch, a grilled cheese sandwich at Kenny & Zuke's Deli, her phone told her that the cameras had recorded movement. She drove to St. Johns to notarize some papers for a tire company. Then she photographed an undamaged Mack truck its owner was claiming had been totaled.

When she finally made it to the bar through Portland's increasingly aggravating traffic to check the camera feed, she was ready for a real drink. Nursing her Stoli & 7 (it was on the cuff – Burt *had* said he wanted to pay full freight), she ran through the recordings on her tablet.

They had fired twice when Burt visited the basement to restock. The third recording was more of a puzzle. The shape showing up in the infrared video was hazy and indistinct, while cameras two and three just showed unrelieved darkness. She wondered for a few moments if the motion-activated cameras had malfunctioned, or whether a mouse had tripped them.

Then a blob, human in shape and size, reared up in camera one. It was no normal person. Its heat signature registered as a cold spot against the chill background of the basement, clearly a female profile. Whoever – or whatever – it was maneuvered easily in the dark. Then, the shape simply blinked off after being on-screen for nineteen seconds. She moved the slider back to the left and watched the transition again. The time stamp showed the recordings had been made just before two in the morning.

Casey retrieved the key from Burt and went downstairs to check the setup. Everything seemed in order and there were no signs of anyone having disturbed the cameras. She shaded her eyes as the second and third cameras' bright lights came on, indicating they were recording her. A shiver went through her that had nothing to do with the temperature.

The door at the top of the stairs slammed shut. Someone had to have closed it. Casey froze, straining to listen. A sharp click told her the hasp had been thrown on the other side of the door. The camera lights and the overhead both went off, plunging the room into darkness. Her attention snapped to her remaining senses -- she heard a scraping behind her. Who knew she was coming down here? What did they want of *her*?

Slowly, Casey pulled her phone from her pocket. She pushed a button and soft light suffused the room. She wished she were carrying her Glock. What good was it doing her locked in the gun safe in her closet? She pointed the lighted screen at the stairs above her but it showed nothing. No one was there. Casey relied on logic and clear rules – when something was scraping on the stairs above you in the dark, it had to be there when the light is on them. She turned around.

Where there had been a pile of debris blocking the archway to the tunnels at the back of the basement, now there was an open doorway framed by wooden beams. The wood looked newer than she expected in this old basement, and shining her light upwards she found that the beams over her head also looked less ancient. Shoe prints, female ones with high heels, now showed up leading right through it. Her light was absorbed by the blackness beyond. Casey told herself she really ought to go up the stairs and bang on the door until somebody opened it. Any reasonable person would. Casey was reasonable. She glanced at her phone: no service but plenty of battery left. She kept having to thumb the screen to keep the light going.

She was halfway up the stairs when a voice came faintly from the new doorway. "Help. Somebody. Please!"

"Dana?"

"Casey? Please!"

Biting her lower lip, Casey felt a momentary flash of terror race up her back. Then it transformed into fear for Dana, and something else. An obligation. It was her fault Dana was down here; she'd brought her to the Castaway, had led her on, had served her just when she was most vulnerable.

"Oh, babe. How long have you been here?" She followed the voice back down the stairs. At the bottom she pulled a heavy champagne bottle out of an open case. It was no nine-mil but it was better than nothing.

The tunnel's ceiling hung even lower than the basement's had been. Casey had to bend her knees and duck-walk to stay under it with her head up. The air got cooler every step she took but Dana's voice seemed fainter the farther she went.

"No-o-o-o!" Dana cried out, her voice still more distant but louder. Fear resonated in her voice like it hadn't before. Then everything fell silent.

A voice sounded, but it seemed to originate inside her ears rather than in the room around her.

Go away. The voice was her dead mother's. *Who is*

this one to you? No. It sounded like her mom, but her mother would never have called anybody "this one."

"Dana!" Casey shouted. Her voice seemed to be sucked up by the darkness, just like her light. A shiver ran through her now, even though the air still and musty, the space was claustrophobically tight. "Who are you?" she shouted without really wanting to hear the answer.

I'm so lonely. Her mother's voice. Almost. The voice wanted to sound like her mother's. It changed tactics. *Come, join this one.*

Casey reminded herself it was not her mom. It was important that she keep that straight. Why? She felt overcome by the urge to follow the voice deeper into the tunnel network, to find her dead mother waiting for her. *Am I dreaming this?*

She moved forward, toward the voice. The tunnel t-ed. A faint whimper came from the right, clearly outside herself and not a dream. As Casey stooped along, the ceiling gradually rose, ending in a room holding an antique roll-top desk, a broken chair, and a pallet on the floor with a very real Dana Palace lying on it.

"Please," said Dana, shading her eyes from the light on Casey's phone. "Are you real this time?"

"As real as you are," Casey said, not fully certain how real any of this was. She crouched to put a hand on the other woman's shoulder, putting the bottle on the floor.

NO! The voice sounded not at all like her mother now.

Casey ignored it. "Come on, let's get you out of here."

"I was just trying to get away from you," whispered Dana as she pulled herself up, wiping tears away with her hand. "The door to the basement was open, so I went that way to see if I could get out. There was an open door down there. But as soon as I went through, it went dark. I started to feel my way around, looking for that door, but I couldn't see my hand in front of my nose and all I could find was concrete and brick walls. I've been down here ever since."

Casey didn't stop to answer. She waved around her phone, casting the light around in the direction she had come – the wall facing her was solid, no sign of the opening she had just walked through. A moment of vertigo came over her.

Dana pointed back the way Casey had come. From her widened eyes, it was obvious she had heard, or felt something, as well. "No," she cried, "don't let it happen again!" A faint shimmer, like a heat mirage, occupied the center of the room.

"Again? What is it?" When she turned, Casey saw that the chair and desk were in different corners than she remembered. They looked newer, less dusty.

I was abandoned. But now we are together, for always, said the voice, so familiar, soft, reassuring like her mother's had been, yet different. Dana's eyes got even bigger, if that were possible.

"Did you hear that?" Casey asked.

"Yes! Inside my head. It sounded just like you."

The apparition began forming, a womanly shape inside a swirl of glowing light, like the tip of a cigar swinging wildly, with a slowly fading orange nimbus. A woman, wrapped in a flowing diaphanous gown, occupied the center of the light show.

The voice, no longer disguised as her mother's, rang from within Casey's ears. *How long now? So many days.* The voice now sounded more plaintive than threatening. *I have been alone for so long.*

"Years," Casey said. "By the look of things I don't think anyone's been down here for decades." The swirl of color deepened momentarily. In that instant Casey could just make out the face of a young Asian woman, a black braid hanging over her shoulder. Then it melted into the darkness again. Dana stood beside her, transfixed, soundless.

I came to America with my brother. Our family could not afford to feed everyone and they sent us off. Girls and women were not allowed, so he smuggled me in. My brother promised me he would see I was well taken care of but work was hard to find for a Chinese man, let alone his unworthy little sister.

The translucent woman stopped talking, or the words stopped forming in Casey's head, and she buried her face in ghostly hands. Casey had seen that move so many times, in the interrogation room when the perp finally realized he was going to confess, when a girl was ready to admit she'd been assaulted. Whether they deserved it or not, it was shame. It always preceded a confession.

He sold me to a white man. I became a...a concubine for whoever would pay his price. I was so shamed! I ran away. But there was nowhere to go. Nowhere in the city could I find a home – she indicated the gown with a sweep of her arms – *dressed like this.*

Chinese women were banned in America; I was afraid of what would happen to me if I were found. Some of the other women said that men were taken from bars sometimes, dragged through tunnels under the buildings to ships bound for Shanghai. I thought if I could make my way through, I could hide on one of those ships until it was out at sea. I could go home again. But I could not find my way to a ship. I had no food, nothing to drink. I was afraid I would be beaten if I went back upstairs, so I just kept looking.

All at once the unreality, the impossibility of what she was seeing and hearing crashed in on Casey. She'd never believed in the supernatural, not since she'd left home and church. In college, in a dozen years on the force, in the years since as a PI, everything she'd experienced had a natural explanation. She'd scoffed at ghost-hunting television shows, even as she watched them through to the end credits. Now, when faced with a specter, she realized none of those shows had prepared her for what to do when she found one.

Dana sobbed loudly, breaking Casey's spell. That was real. She turned on the phone's camera and swung her arm in a wide arc, taking in the doorway, the desk, and the chair, all showing clearly on the screen, all where they had been when she entered. The ghost had difficulty fooling modern devices. Good to know.

She grabbed Dana by the sleeve and walked calmly through the middle of the room. Holding the phone out stiff-armed in front of her, she stepped toward the bricks without hesitating as they passed through the swirling lights around the lost Chinese prostitute.

Then the phone died. In pitch darkness, Casey felt dizzy, disoriented, no longer able to say with any certainty whether she was moving straight ahead. Finding a wall, she felt along it but found no door. She tightened her grip on Dana's arm and whispered reassurances that she wished she believed more herself.

I have been so lonely. For so long, the voice intoned inside Casey's head.

"No," Dana shouted. "Don't do this to us!"

Decades, you say, the voice intoned. *Alone. Forever alone. But now, alone no longer.*

That caught Casey in the gut. She knew what loneliness was, knew it as a hole deep within. It was an absence shaped like her mother, and like the partner whose death had haunted her, even after she had resigned from the force. The hole she had felt she might be able to fill again when she'd first laid eyes on Dana. The loneliness that she had reaffirmed as her own when she'd pushed the manila envelope across the table.

Casey's mind raced. The ghost did not feel malicious. But she was unhinged enough to keep Dana and her down here until they died of dehydration. Then their shades might, perhaps, join hers.

Casey didn't have any physical resources; the bottle was useless against a phantasm, the phone was disabled, if she'd had her gun it would have been just as ineffective. All she had was left was her brain, her determination. And her word.

"I can fix your loneliness," she said to the darkness. "I promise. Just let us go. I promise I won't forget."

There was a long pause. Beside her Dana stirred. "Casey?"

"Wait."

They stood in darkness for what seemed forever. Then the air around her felt a little less chill. The door that hadn't been there a moment before now appeared, limned in a dim glow from the tunnel's end. She ushered Dana through it quickly, afraid it would be shrouded in darkness again in another instant. From the other side of the threshold, she turned and asked the spirit her name.

I am Chang Ming Li. It was the faintest of whispers in her head. *Remember me.*

Armed with the name, Casey unearthed the immigration records and eventually some family in Yunnan province. Building inspectors explored the tunnels and declared them safe. An archeology class from Portland State jumped at the chance to map the underground system and dug under the piles of refuse. Casey was not surprised that no other remains were found.

Casey contacted a Taoist priest about having Ming Li's bones repatriated for burial in her home village. After burning incense in the tunnel and practicing Fu Ji, automatic writing in the ashes, he advised her to let the spirit spend some happy years in the Yang Jian - the earthly realm - before sending her on to Yin Jian and her next life.

***

Burt pulled a chair up to Casey's table. He sat, passing her a double of her regular. Shifting to one side, he tugged an envelope out of a rear pocket. He slid it her way. "Your fee, plus expenses, as invoiced."

"Thanks, Burt," she said, tucking the envelope into her purse sight unseen. Lord knows she could use it. Seems like every bill in the world came due at the same time.

She looked around. The Castaway was packed. Ephraim, newly promoted from maintenance to tour guide, gathered the tourists up and led them to the newly refurbished back of the bar to start the Ghost Tunnel tour. The man had unplumbed acting chops.

"Congrats, Burt," said Casey. "The bar's doing well and our resident ghost will have plenty of company." She sipped her drink and put the half-full glass on the table as she stood. She held out a hand. "Goodbye, Burt."

He looked puzzled. "It's always been 'See you later.' What's this 'goodbye' stuff, Doll?"

"No offense, but when your best friend is a bartender, it's a bad sign."

Casey smiled and looked toward the door, where Dana stood waiting for her, uncertainty vying with determination on her face. "I've got a second date."

Metamorphose: The Dark Door
Tanya Fillbrook

Just like an emerald green butterfly emerging from its cocoon, sticky, left like a filigree leaf floating in the garden room. Alice became more than flesh and blood.
Alice pressed against the glass of a pane and reviewed her transformation, her large treacle-colored peepers adjusting to the shortness of her lightyears.
Two days, maybe two more years; who knows except for that life of colour I spy from my window, out of my reach yet into my dreams.
And I think of my moth girl.

My ornate mirror turns my face into wrinkles and warts, and the flushed cheeks I once remembered have now become like a paste filling creamed with hopelessness.
Will Alice remember me now?
Will she hold my hand as I retell stories of great summers and playful Winters frolicking in white icing sugar snow?
My pencils tell my story, sketching out cryptid space wings made to fly. From my womb, a chrysalis in astronomical time, late, yet perfectly formed made behind the dark door, created or so I thought from a feeling known as "love."

It hurts me when I breathe out toxins from the radon poisoning and my muscles appear misplaced somehow.
I'm metamorphosing into something bigger: a new phase through a lens of tinsel town and the blue starscape above my eye view flickers like dots of paint-wash stinking of melting plastic.
I am soaring somewhere across the Milky Way.
My pounding soundtrack takes me back to before I became a work in progress; a trial of some sort when I was taken to this one ship and left to give birth without Tristan by my side, and Alice with no father to recall. A Gothic creation indeed is one of beauty yet still with simple flaws but nothing like a beast of flesh with humanoid distinction, but my Alice is delicate with wings that will

not beat here in the darkest backdrop of space and time but instead rise to each hum I produce for her alert hearing.

I will tend to her needs and feed her plant juice and fungi spores and hope she will be strong enough to be invited through the dark door where she will thrive through moth lights and then in the warmth of her surroundings live to become fully-grown Alice will then use her wings to spread her message to a prospective populace.
This journey I did not choose. I came here to be an engineer-the person ready to extend the shell worlds for the new arrivals in the forthcoming fifty years, yet instead I was tricked into a dark coma of fear and germination to commence the moth dance and become a cryptid cripple of sorts. I suppose I can be thankful for my life, one superseding that of just a few days. I Pray for my Alice wishing her longevity and some serenity here in the quiet world.

I love you, Alice.

Alice jiggers about as my Goth-Punk vibes pop around the landing dock just for her as I take time to replenish my stock. Her favorite cherry nectar which she needs to flourish will be smelled by her as soon as the heat lamps are fixed up.

The cherry nectar whiffs across the darkened room and attracts both newborns and adults alike. I take one plant delicately chosen for her growth and without hesitation, she draws out the juicy nectar from inside and I can see her glee.

My humanoid hands take hold of lacy wings and I caress her close to me.
She is ready.

I watch the mammoth transformation of my daughter moth into my daughter complete with limbs made to rap against the toughest of them all-the Avengers. Those that wish to be done away with us once the cycle has been completed. How are we to be exterminated, I ask myself. I will fight my last breath for us to go together wherever our last destination is.

We wait in limbo through the dark door together and her large black eyes tell me her new story about us as one complete unit as a changeling from one to another. She buries her long black mane of hair into my arms and she sobs for fear of her fate.

As we listen intently, eyes ever larger we hear the moans of the moths with empty bellies, starving in fact, and making their way to my Alice still weak from her transformation. I keep her close to me using my powerful wings to bat them out of the way.

But the dark door inside its full interior holds darker secrets. Metamorphosing into cryptids does not allow us freedom but only fattens up the fragile and delicate moth sub-species; very rare indeed and prized by their makers. New science is everything after all.

I hold onto Alice ever tighter but she is gripped by another attaching itself to her extended wing, then another hovers above her head, and another. I can not fend them off as more winged fighters take their places surrounding us until the grow lights fade and the munching begins. There is little left of her, my Alice, I love you!

I feel my antennae attacked and loosened from my head and the biting of moths into my skin and bone.

Fading, fading further I keep hold of a tiny piece of Alice's beautiful laced wing until the dark door behind me becomes infested with new larvae, and I see no more.

Prodigal
R. C. Capasso

"Leeds? Is that on our way?" Deborah stared out of the coach window. Surely they should be traveling southwest.

Jeremy's face twitched in a smile. "Aren't you clever? I meant to keep it a surprise for a little longer."

"A surprise?"

"We're not returning to Nottingham."

Their honeymoon on the wintry coast had been so wonderful, the biting wind off the water buffeting her face, pressing against her body, challenging her to resist it. She had never felt more alive. But tomorrow she expected to see her friends and receive her first calls as Mrs. Jeremy Bretton.

"Not returning?"

"No. I have quite a different home for us."

"A different...?" Her voice slipped away with her breath. "Where are we going?"

"Let me surprise you."

She studied this man she had known for all of five months. Tall and thin, his long hands clasped before him. Dark hair smooth, face clean-shaven, head in profile so that most of the scars faced away from her. Her husband. Her Jeremy.

"But aren't we expected? Your office..."

"Leave that to me. You trust me, don't you?"

"Of course."

He was a creature of surprises, despite his staid demeanor. First pressing to wed so quickly, then their unique honeymoon and now this. She'd never told him she didn't like the unexpected. Maybe it was best she hadn't. Marriage was about adaptation, and perhaps Jeremy's individuality would stretch her, make her less an old maid in her thinking. She would do all she could to adapt.

***

The house loomed above them in the dark. They'd journeyed two long days through rain and sleet. The church bell in the nearby village was striking one a.m. when they arrived. No lights at the doors or in any windows. She blinked sleep from her eyes as Jeremy threw down the reins of the gig he'd hired at the last town.

"Are we expected?"

Jeremy laughed, and she turned. Was this truly the first time she'd heard him laugh? That wasn't possible. But the sound struck her as new, strange.

"They'll know me, even after these years!" He leapt from the gig and moved toward the door. Stiff, pulling her bulky skirts around her, she eased herself to the ground.

He pulled a set of keys from his pocket and in a moment swung the door inward with a creak of hinges. The interior of the house opened before them like a cave, damp, musty and so dark she pulled back as if a mask had been thrust upon her.

Jeremy strode forward, his boots clattering against the floor.

"Hello!" His voice echoed. "The prodigal has returned."

She edged to the doorway and halted as slowly, arms out to his sides, head tilted back as if to drink in the darkness, Jeremy spun on his heels. "Glad to see me?"

She took a step forward out of the wind, then nearly fell backwards as Jeremy brushed past her. For one brief second a ludicrous idea sprang into her mind: he was going to leave, locking here in this horrible place.

But he was only gone a moment, bringing in two of their bags.

"Let's have some light!" His voice bounced off the barren walls as he strode in. She stepped out of his way, knowing somehow he wasn't waiting for her response.

Her feet frozen, her mind benumbed also, she followed him into one room after another as he found and lit lamps. In a drawing room he kicked at an empty hearth. "How cold hearted! Not even a fire for your returning boy? No matter. We'll all be happy together soon. I'm what you want, now."

The few lamps sent bizarre shadows onto the walls and fell on sheet-covered furniture. Over and over her mind tricked her, making her imagine occupants on the veiled chairs. As Jeremy moved, almost dancing, he swept the shadows with him. As if he were not alone.

Deborah returned to the entryway and sank onto the steps leading upward into darkness. She couldn't sit on one of the sofas, a companion to the shadows.

Jeremy dashed past her, pounding up the stairs, still calling to someone. Surely, if there were a caretaker, a servant, anyone waiting for them, they would have been roused. His voice cut through the house, joyful, exuberant. Triumphant.

***

"Aren't you hungry?"

She'd finally roused herself enough to find a kitchen. There was no fresh food, just a few dusty jars of preserves and a box of tea left in the back of a pantry shelf. They must go to a village for provisions if they were going to stay. All she could offer her husband was a pot of tea and remnants of some bread and cheese she'd saved from their last stop at an inn.

"I don't need anything," He barely glanced at her.

"Are we staying? Because if we are..."

He turned large eyes to her, his brow furrowed. "Of course we're staying. This is our home. Uncle Arthur has passed away, and finally the house is mine again."

She took a slow breath. "Are there no servants?" She and Mother had managed alone, but in a house this size and with a husband expecting more of life...

"I've engaged a couple. They're expecting us tomorrow. But I couldn't wait."

Snatching one of her bags, he bounded up the stairs and turned to the right wing. Flinging open a door, he spoke over his shoulder. "You can sleep here." He tossed the bag on the floor, then jogged down the landing to the opposite wing and disappeared into a doorway. When she crept behind to speak to him, she found the door locked. He had retired for the night. She made her way to her icy room and slid between musty sheets.

In the night the house moaned around her, as she buried her face in her pillow and cried.

***

The next day the Jensons arrived. A middle-aged couple, they stood in shock to see the house already occupied, with Deborah struggling to light the kitchen fire. Mrs. Jenson silently waved her aside while Abner, her husband, rushed off to seek Jeremy for his orders.

Deborah watched in silence as furniture emerged from dust cloths, drapes were pulled back, and the house began to come to life. The Jensons worked stolidly, speaking only to each other in brief, low tones, while she moved from room to room to stay out of their way. Jeremy appeared each morning, giving all of them orders, then disappeared up into the long echoing halls of the house.

The first day she tried to follow him, tried to ask for a tour of the property. But he brushed her off, saying she should rest from their trip. At dinner he spoke only of the past, his boyhood, his mother and sister Andrea. How elegant and brilliant they had been.

He instructed Mrs. Jenson to cook only from a cookbook holding his family's favorite meals. He never asked what Deborah preferred, nor did he want her in the kitchen, running the house. At times it seemed as if he wished to erase her from his life.

"I know your mother had modest ways." His smile cut her. "That's over now."

It was Mother's death that brought them together. In those dark days when she could barely function, someone had recommended him as solicitor.

He was particular about everything. "The Bretton house is always full of life. It must all be beautiful. Full of light." He ordered her to fill the vases with flowers, though the only garden she could see from the windows lay overgrown, gray and sodden under the fog and daily lashes of sleet.

"The conservatory, you fool." His voice had an edge.

"Where...?"

"Oh, come then." He'd set off through a large reception chamber, an equally elegant space he called the "music room" and finally past a door into a glassed hothouse.

"We use Mother's collection in winter." Brushing past her, he disappeared down an adjacent hall.

Deborah covered her nose with her hand. The conservatory must have once been beautiful. Plants of all shapes spilled over long tables and climbed up the glass. But the smell of rot nearly drove her back. No one had given water, no one had worked the soil in years. She would go outside and cut what evergreens she could find. Jeremy would not like to be disappointed.

On Sunday she asked to attend church. She'd seen the lean building on the village square. Jeremy, his back to her, eyes fixed on the grounds beyond the window, shrugged. She took the gig. Wind pelted her with crystals of ice, but at least the air was clean. She drew up at the old church, high and narrow, made of the local gray stone. Slipping into a pew at the back, she pressed her chilled fingers together. All she could see of her fellow parishioners were their backs, a cluster of dark bonnets and coats, with most of the men's bare heads white haired or silver.

But the vicar, Reverend Nicolas Sterne, had a warm voice. After the service she waited for the congregation to file out, then stopped at the door to introduce herself. At the mention of the Bretton house, Rev. Sterne raised one eyebrow, then immediately relaxed into a benign calm. "It's good to see new life in the neighborhood."

The small woman beside him stretched out a hand. "Yes, you are most welcome. I'm Amelia Sterne, and if my husband or I can do anything for you, please let us know. You'll come to tea this week, perhaps? We're in the parsonage." She gestured to a cottage.

Deborah took a breath. "I should love to come, if I can."

"Your husband, too, of course. We must have you both to dinner."

Deborah lowered her glance. "I will certainly ask my husband."

As Deborah turned the horse from the church, she held the reins with an easier grasp. Faint sunlight broke through the pewter clouds, and the wind was at her back now. She'd been right to come to church. Now she knew two good and solid people to be her allies.

Allies? What a strange thought. She had no enemy, so how could she need an alliance?

Yet as the gig neared the house, her chest began to tighten again. How dark it seemed, how cold and forbidding under any light.

***

Stepping inside, the atmosphere felt different. For an instant she thought that someone had come to visit. But there was no cart, no horse. Perhaps someone walked over the moor?

She entered the parlor, immediately struck by the smell of lavender. Three glasses stood on a side table. But Jeremy sat alone, leaning back against a chair beside the fire.

"Has someone visited?"

"Just a quiet day at home."

On an impulse she reached her hand down to touch his face, the side with the scars. His hand struck hers at the wrist, pushing it away as he stood and brushed past her.

"Don't. My face made me what I had to be. Sober. Respectable. But I hate it." He kept his back to her, rigid. As she held her breath he forced his shoulders to relax. He half turned, showing only his unmarked skin. "Don't remind me of it. Never again."

Her body almost rocked under the tension, and she took a step back to steady herself. Blindly she cast about for something normal to say. "I met the vicar. Nicholas Sterne and his wife Amelia. Do you know them?"

Jeremy shrugged.

"They've invited me to tea. Perhaps I could ask them to call here also?" Her heart pounded as if she'd proposed some atrocity.

It took a long moment for Jeremy to respond. When he smiled, she instinctively looked away.

"Perfect," he said.

***

Overnight it snowed. Stepping down to the empty dining room, she couldn't fight a sigh. Jeremy never took breakfast with her, nor lunch. All day he left her alone as he rambled somewhere in the house or on the grounds. But would he have gone out so early on such a frigid day?

She moved to the window and caught her breath. Jeremy passed a few yards ahead of her, bareheaded, without a coat, walking lightly as if the snow didn't drag at his boots. He would catch his death.

Shocked, she ran for a shawl and hurried out the front steps. Jeremy had disappeared around the far corner, perhaps heading for the gardens or the park, and she ploughed forward, slipping in the fresh snow, gasping as it covered her light shoes and tugged at her skirts. His footprints were obvious in the softly mounding drifts. A light easy stride, careless in the snow.

And beside them another pair. Smaller. A woman's footprints, the marks of a light shoe, a dancing slipper.

But she had seen no one beside Jeremy.

A few yards on, and another set of prints appeared. A woman's shoes, with the sweep of skirts dragging behind them.

She stood motionless as wind spat crystals of snow into her face. Gulping the freezing air, she turned to run. Back into the house, into the warmth, her wet feet slipping on the smooth tiles.

She raced across the foyer through parlor and dining room and to the back of the music room, where windows looked out onto the wintry garden.

Jeremy paced alone, gesturing, but one arm held at his waist as if someone's hand gripped it lightly as they walked. Through the icy glass she heard his voice softly talking and laughing.

She barely realized she had climbed to her room until she laid her shawl on the bed and sank down beside it.

Later, when Jeremy came in for lunch, his hands and face were red, but he didn't seem to feel the cold. He sat without a word and ate heartily.

Did they come into the house with him, the beings that walked beside him in the snow?

***

"I hope your husband is well." Amelia Sterne offered a cup of tea.

"Yes, he is fine." Deborah's mind blanked. She hardly knew how to speak of him.

"We're encouraged that he has come back to the neighborhood. A solicitor and married, just as his family wanted."

Deborah made herself take a sip of milky tea. "You knew him when he was younger?"

"Only slightly. My husband was new in his appointment, and he called on the family. But they were going through a difficult time, and we never had much contact. Then your husband, quite a young man at the time, left the area. A few weeks later the rest of the family became ill and passed away quite quickly, one after the other. The father, mother and the daughter."

"An illness?"

Amelia's brow wrinkled. "I believe so."

"Was it...?" Deborah could see Jeremy's face. "Small pox?"

Amelia shook her head firmly. "No. Our community never suffered an outbreak. I believe your husband contracted the malady in London. I think his family...oh, but it doesn't matter now."

"What about his family?"

"They had concerns about some of the connections he formed when he was studying in London."

"What kind of connections?"

"I couldn't really say. There was a young woman, I think."

When Deborah turned her head, Amelia reddened. "I'm sorry. I'm sure she meant nothing. I don't want to gossip. The essential thing is that your husband is making a new start."

"Yes." Deborah sipped at the cold tea. "He calls himself a prodigal."

***

She sat at her dressing table, staring into her reflection. She had never been a beauty. She was well past the age of a blushing bride when Jeremy chose her. But now her cheeks were pale, her eyes encircled with darkness. No wonder he barely looked at her.

A light tap on her door made her jump. Jeremy? She stood at once and hurried to open to him.

Mrs. Jenson stood in the doorway, hands gripping her apron.

"Begging your pardon, Madam. But could I have a word with you?"

Deborah stepped back and admitted her. A brief gesture of the cook's hand made her close the door. Jeremy hated to see her in contact with the servants.

They faced one another awkwardly.

"It's just this, Madam. I was at Carson's store today, getting our groceries, and Mr. Carson told me something."

Deborah waited.

"He says the Master was at the store, ordering things for his mother and sister. Gloves, fabric, lotions, hairpins. More than once the Master said it was for them, so Carson took notice."

Deborah's chest tightened. "Mr. Carson must have understood. Perhaps my husband means a surprise for me."

Mrs. Jenson's face twisted slightly. "Mrs. Carson and Jenny Talbert heard the same thing. You know...." She looked away. "You know things aren't right. Abner and me, we can't stay here."

Deborah's hand came to her throat. "We're giving a dinner for the Sternes on Friday. You have to stay for that."

The cook's face softened. "All right. I know. But no more after that. You'll have to find someone else."

***

Deborah's breath rasped as she nearly fell in the yard. Snow and slush gave under at her boots, making her skid. No control over her body. No control over anything. She climbed into the gig and drove away, Jenson staring after her.

The horse was struggling up the slick hill when they met an oncoming gig.

"Mrs. Bretton?" The vicar pulled up short.

"Reverend Sterne. I was coming to see you or Amelia."

"Is something wrong?"

Deborah gripped the reins. "I'm worried about my husband. If there's anything you know, please tell me."

Sterne dropped his reins and descended, climbing into the gig to sit beside her.

"What's happened?"

"I don't know. He seems to be living in the past." She could not speak of the things living with them. "Memories of his family are affecting him somehow." She took a breath. "What do you know of him?"

Sterne frowned but met her eyes. "I've heard your husband had a troubled youth. Expelled from a couple of schools, and they couldn't keep a tutor to work with him at home. His father became increasingly severe. When Jeremy fell ill in London, the old man claimed he led a wild life and disowned him. Jeremy tried to come back but was shut out."

Deborah faced into the wind to stare back at the grim, brooding house. "And his mother, his sister?"

Sterne gave a helpless shrug. "I think they wanted your husband to come home to them, but they couldn't act against the old man. And I believe they were a little frightened of Jeremy, the wildness of his manner. A month later the family all died within hours of one another. Jeremy didn't attend the funeral."

Deborah's chest throbbed. "Was there an inquest?"

Sterne swallowed. "No. Our physician was old, beyond fighting. There was talk, but no investigation. Jeremy was gone, no one knew where. The old man left the house to his brother, who only came here for one day, to close it up."

They both turned to stare toward the village. The houses facing together for safety, the church like a guardian. The snow-covered graveyard stretched toward them.

Sterne laid his hand on Deborah's. "Do you want to come stay with us for a time? I could call on your husband."

Deborah couldn't say, "He's no husband to me." She couldn't say what she suspected, what she knew, or there'd be a doctor coming for her.

And she would not leave Jeremy. Not when he needed so much.

***

The house was quiet when she returned. Mrs. Jenson worked in the kitchen, her face stony. Deborah scanned the first floor for Jeremy, but the rooms stood empty. She trembled to look for his footprints outside.

She climbed the staircase and halted at the top. His wing of the house was silent, the hall heavy in shadow from all the closed doors. Only the far window at the end sent a bleak winter light that died within a few feet.

A spark seemed to burst in her chest. She shouldn't be living like this. Jeremy had no right to keep her closed away in an odious, frightful house with no companionship, no word of love or tender touch.

Her skirts rustled as she hurried to his door.

"Jeremy!" She tapped and waited. No stirring inside. She knocked again, louder, and then grasped the doorknob. It wouldn't turn. Why should he lock the door? What did he think of her, that he must lock her out?

She pounded the wood again and heard a creak. The door of the next room opened slowly, sending a ghostly light across the floor. Her breath caught in her throat, but she moved forward. Perhaps it was his dressing room and he was coming out to her.

But no one stood in the doorway. She stared across a woman's bedroom, with a dress laid out on the bed. Risking one step in, she hugged her arms as cold wrapped around her. The room could have been a tomb abandoned for years. Yet on the dressing table lay an open bottle of lotion.

A faint movement of air and the soft rub of wood on wood meant another door had opened. She turned, her body stiff. Not Jeremy's chamber, but the room opposite. And then down the hall, door after door swinging open. From one room came the sound of a music box. From another the creak of a chair.

She could barely lift her feet, numb as if she'd stood for hours in the enveloping cold. She made herself glance into each chamber. Three occupied; it seemed as if at any moment someone would step out, laughing, calling. Yet all were deadly silent.

She dug her nails into her arms, trying to stop shaking. The thin winter light made smudged shadows, strange tricks from odd angles, so that her own shade seemed multiplied, baffling her.

At the end of the hall the light of the far window dimmed, slowly blotted out. A shadow seemed to be growing against the light, but it couldn't be hers. She was too far away. And it was so high, high and broad. Looming to fill the window, deepening, thickening to almost fleshly consistency.

A man. Not Jeremy. Taller, towering.

"Mr. Jenson!" The words broke from her stiffened lips.

The shape moved toward her.

"Mr. Jenson!" Anger made the words sharp, loud.

"Yes, Madam?"

His answer came faintly. Behind her. Below her.

Backing away, her eyes filling with the darkness as it drew ever closer, Deborah stumbled. She stretched a hand out behind her, as if she were blind.

"Madam?"

A hand closed round hers, small, smooth and cold. Pulling her back.

With a cry she shook it off and fled down the hall, stopping to catch herself at the top of the landing.

Gripping the balustrade, she stared down.

Jenson looked up at her, his face pale. "Can I help you, Madam?"

She stumbled to the stairs, eyes unseeing. The first step disappeared under her, space opened up, and she lurched forward.

Something, someone caught her by the arms, pulling her. Jerking her till she fell back against the wall.

She clung to the banister, a great sob cracking open her breast, flooding her with breath.

Jenson leapt up the steps toward her, but she was safe. She had her balance back. She hadn't fallen; it had stopped her.

Someone or something unseen had saved her from her panic, from the dark shadow.

There was more than one of them.

***

She stood at the bottom of the stairs as the gig arrived. She'd chosen her best dress, the one she wore the night Jeremy asked for her hand. She didn't expect Jeremy to remember.

He advanced to greet the vicar and his wife. Rev. Sterne extended his hand with a warm smile.

"We've met before, you know, sir."

"Oh, I remember. I remember everything." Jeremy looked around the foyer. "It's so good to have the house alive again. All of us together." He burst into a laugh, as Rev. Sterne took a half step back.

They moved to the drawing room. Jeremy almost danced from one to another, motioning everyone to seats, offering sherry. He seemed ten years younger, even teasing Mrs. Sterne, who turned large silent eyes upon him. Deborah sank into a chair at the edge of the group, refusing a glass. Her stomach tensed, watching Jeremy as if she'd never seen him before.

Jenson announced that dinner was served.

Jeremy gallantly offered his arm to Mrs. Sterne, who took it calmly. Rev. Sterne came to Deborah's side, sending her a quick glance as if to say, "Steady on."

Jeremy held a chair for Mrs. Sterne on the far side of the table when Deborah entered and halted.

The table was set for seven. She'd prepared for four. Mrs. Jenson knew they were to be four. Yet Jeremy was waving her and Rev. Sterne to places that left both ends of the table free.

"Well, come on!" He laughed and glanced toward the empty doorway. "I'll be quite embarrassed in a moment!"

The candles flickered as a cool breeze passed over the table. Deborah looked to the drapes, but they were tightly closed.

"That's better." Jeremy moved to the far end of the table. "Mother, you are beautiful as ever."

He pulled out a chair beside Rev. Sterne. "You know my sister, of course."

The vicar pushed his chair back. "Mr. Bretton, let's just step into the drawing room."

"The drawing room!" Jeremy laughed, then his face tightened. "Don't be a fool, man. We're about to have dinner."

Rev. Sterne's face paled. "Jeremy, let's just take a moment."

"For prayer, padre? That's hardly necessary. I have all I want." He stretched out his arms. "My family together again. The prodigal returned home. The fatted calf." He laughed again, gesturing toward Mrs. Jenson who halted in the door from the kitchen, a tureen in her hands.

"I'm forgiven, you know. Mother and Andrea have given their blessing. I'm their boy again. No more misbehavior. Even a nice little safe wife to show I've reformed." Jeremy waved a hand toward Deborah, his eyes never turning toward her. "They've taken me back. They love me."

Rev. Sterne reached one hand forward as if to touch his arm, but Jeremy backed away.

'You remember, of course. All you worthy old men. Like my father."

He rounded the table, bumping the back of Mrs. Sterne's seat as he moved to jerk out the chair from the head of the table.

"Father! I know you're here."

The candles from the table blew out. The open doorway and the kitchen door, ajar where Mrs. Jenson stood frozen, gave the only light, casting weird shadows onto the walls.

"Come on, Father! Give us your blessing. I've done everything you wanted. I've changed my ways. I've built the dreary profession you wanted. I've married the little mouse you'd have chosen."

Deborah couldn't even move to cover her face.

"I don't see anyone anymore. My friends are all dead or gone." He raised a hand and covered his scars. "We can go back to what we were. You can come back."

A keening sounded, starting low, almost indistinguishable under his voice, then rising. Mrs. Jenson bolted back into the kitchen, the door closing, leaving them deeper in darkness, while Amelia began a soft prayer.

"Bretton, get hold of yourself." Sterne strode forward and gripped Jeremy by one arm.

"Get off me!" Jeremy shoved him away and darted around the table toward the door. He whirled and pointed a shaking hand at the pastor.

"You've no right to reject me, Father. I've done everything you want, and now you have to accept me." His face twisted, eyes gleaming. "You know what happened when you refused me. You know what I can do."

He turned and ran. The vicar dashed after him as Deborah fought her way from the table, her skirt catching at her feet.

She was two steps into the foyer when she saw him leaping up the stairway, stopping at the landing. Shadows streaked across the walls. Jeremy's figure, long and distorted. Other shades, too, cast from some unknown light, moving independently. Moving almost knowingly, purposefully around him.

"Take me back!" he shouted. "You have to take me back. I won't go on without you. I belong here."

Sterne crept up the stairs, back gliding along the wall.

"Take me back! I've come back to you!"

Sterne was two steps away, his hands stretching out, when Jeremy froze. Staring at something before him in the darkness, he slowly dipped his head.

Before Sterne could grab him, he was over the railing, falling to the marble floor.

Deborah screamed as hands gripped her.

"Don't look!" Amelia's voice sounded miles off.

But she pulled away and threw herself onto the floor, the velvet dress spilling around her. "Andrea, help him!" The words tore from her throat.

For an instant Jeremy's eyes flicked open, staring past her. "You have to take me back now, Father." His eyes closed.

They pulled her outside into the cold clean snowy night until she stopped screaming. The house stood in darkness, its questions silenced, its waiting done.

Paranormal Abyss
Denny E. Marshall

Shortly after death
Spend mystic lifetime dreaming
That you're alive
In room size of universe
Endless array of small beds

The Coral Spas
Daniel Crow

"Do you know what you're being punished for, God's slave Vasiliy Korsikov?" Father Grigori, a tall man in a battered black robe with white inscriptions, thundered, towering over the man tied to the log. Seryoga's uncle only had his pants on, his back exposed.

"Yes," *Dyadya* Vasya said, his voice grimmer than usual. "We were blast-fishing too close to the Coral Spas. We could have hurt the reef."

"Jesus, what idiots," Seryoga whispered to me. "Vasya and Igor, his *koresh*... Just wanna get drunk and blow shit up, always."

"Do you realize the gravity of your transgression?" Father Grigori's voice rolled over the small crowd that had gathered in the village center to watch the punishment. "Do you understand what you could have done?"

"I do. I do. I accept... My punishment."

Vasya's voice almost broke at those words. The priest nodded and rolled up his sleeves, then reached for the whip that one of the kids passed to him. A few years ago – I think I was 11 back then – I got to pass him that whip too. Father Grigori didn't do such things too often, but when he did, it was a spectacle that drew all of Severniy Spassk.

An hour later, after *Dyadya* Vasya, agonizing and bloodied, was dragged away to the village doctor, Seryoga and I settled under the apple tree in our garden. I got back to work on my carving, while Seryoga watched Mom water the tomatoes.

"I know where Vasya keeps his dynamite," he whispered. "Wanna go steal a stick or two some day? For shits and giggles?"

"I dunno," I wasn't really listening, putting a cut after cut on the wood. What were her eyes like? Almond-shaped, I think, or maybe round? Hell, so hard to recall...

"Hey, is that a face?" my friend asked, looking at the small carving. "A girl, huh? Is that the one you saw in the city?"

"Yeah," I tried to play it cool, but my cheeks turned crimson. "That's her, ugh..."

"*Tili-tili testo!*" Seryoga shouted, grabbing the tiny wooden plate from my hands. I threw myself at him, but he dodged my bear hug, hopping off the bench, and stuck out his tongue. "She your girlfriend now? Gonna marry here, huh? City gal falling for a *derevenschina* like you?"

"Hey, give it back!" I screamed, charging at him with my fists, but he dodged again, fast as the wind, his stupid laugh ringing in my ears. "She's not my girlfriend!"

"Of course she's not," he laughed, hopping around with the carving in his hands. "Hey, how 'bout I tell your Mom? *Tyotya* Sveta, Mikhei's got a girlfriend!.."

"Don't you dare!" I chased after him as he rushed to the tomato patch.

"What's the noise?" Mom looked angry. Seryoga knew how to be an annoying devil, and it only got worse since his parents started to homeschool him. "If you got nothing to do, Sergei, I can find a chore for you – wanna go paint the fence?"

"*Tyotya* Sveta, Misha's got a girlfriend!" he sneered, waving the carving at her like crazy. "A city girl! He's gonna marry her and leave Spassk, he says they'll live in Moscow!"

"Mom, Mom, that's lies, don't listen to him!"

"*Gluposti*," Mom sighed, wiping sweat off her wrinkled forehead, then looked at me and smiled. "Don't fall for city girls, Mikhail, they're not worth it... When you're old enough, we'll find you a good gal here. And Moscow — they're all corrupt criminals there, haven't you heard what Father Grigori says? Stay in Severniy Spassk. Home is where you belong."

***

I was hoping that the girl would show up again, but couldn't catch sight of her all morning, and couldn't leave the stall for long either. We, Severno-Spasskiye, bundled together in the far end of the market, some selling fruits and veggies, others, like me and Mom, bringing more interesting stuff. Carved fish bones, carved wood, carved anything.

Dad was a master carver, and after a bad flu took him to the Coral Spas, his skill hadn't faded one bit. At first, he would come back home every now and then, and we'd sit on the bench under the apple tree carving stuff together. His strong, confident cuts didn't as much create shapes on wood as much as they brought them out of it, as if they had always been there, hidden from anyone but him. I was never as good, but maybe, with time... Maybe.

I was actually pretty proud of the carving I made for the girl, though. I saw her just once, last time I went with Mom to the city, and it was like seeing an angel — not the fat small kids from the icons in the Coral Spas, but the kind that actually make you believe there's more to life than a tiny boring village by the cold sea.

It wasn't a busy day — it never was for me and Mom — and I spaced out every now and then, dreaming of this bigger life. Maybe, she'll love the carving, I thought, and maybe, one day, we'll get to see Moscow together. Maybe, it's not just thugs and thieves there, as Father Grigori says. For him, everything outside Severniy Spassk is just mud and scum, that's why so few people ever leave... That, and the church too.

Dad and I still carved together, just not as often. I didn't really like to go to the church, and he didn't really go out. He wasn't turning into a cold one, at least, not yet. He only faded a bit, and then a bit more. One day, he'd join the crowd at the burner, I knew, and so would anyone we see off to the Coral Spas. Maybe, that's when we'd go to Moscow, me and this girl, when both Mom and Dad would be crawling to the burner on the rock over the village at night to devour its flame...

Maybe... Maybe.

***

Two weeks passed before I saw her again, the girl from my carving. She was with two friends, a lanky guy in a pop band T-shirt, and another girl, a short brunette in fat glasses. Together, they wandered around the market, snatching a snack here and there when nobody was looking.

I didn't hesitate for a moment, making my way through the thin crowd. Her auburn mane was my guiding star in all the greyness around: The gray asphalt beneath us, the gray people walking from stall to stall, and the gray northern sky above.

"*Privet!*" I said confidently, reaching in my pocket for the carving. She turned to face me, her freckles shining like a dozen little suns, and as warm as they were, I still froze in place. I had some idea of what I was going to say — say my name, maybe, or give her the carving, or something witty, but I just lost my breath, like a fish cast ashore. Even worse, the stupid carving got stuck in my pocket, and I pulled harder and harder, trying to release it.

"*Privet*," she said, looking a bit confused. Her brunette friend giggled, and the kid in the T-shirt grinned. "What's up?"

I grinned like an idiot, desperately looking for words. At least the carving, now lovingly polished and glazed, gave way, leaving my pocket — and leaving a hole in it, too.

"Is it for me?" she asked, giggling.

"Dashka, it's you!" her friend gasped. "Wow, it's like... A portrait or something?"

"Yes, it's a portrait," I finally managed to regain my voice. "It's for you. I'm Mikhei, by the way."

"I am Dasha," she smiled, making me blush. "We're hanging here before a movie, Mikhei, wanna see it with us?.."

***

"We're gonna be in the same class," I said. "She said she was in another school, but moving to mine this September 'cause of some bullies. And her Dad's taking her to Turkey this month, to the sea..."

"We got sea here too," Seryoga nodded at the gray waters stretching all the way to the horizon. On days like these, it was hard to tell between the sea and the sky, they were both gray and endless; Only the Coral Spas, the small wooden church on top of the coldwater reef, stood to mark which was which.

"Yeah, but it's cold here. And she's got a dog, they took in a stray one from the streets. Called him Bobik. She says Bobik's a very good boy, they'll leave him with the neighbors when they're gone..."

"My neighbors also had a dog," Seryoga said, looking at the sea. "Sharik, he was old and scruffy. He died last week — the cold ones took him."

"The cold ones?" I asked. "Don't they all gather round the burner at night?"

"One must have gone astray," Seryoga shrugged. "They kept all the doors locked, as you do at night, but Sharik somehow got out in the backyard... And the cold one must have seen him. I saw the corpse, it was covered in ice. Poor Sharik."

"Poor Sharik. Think Father Grigori will let them take him there?" I pointed at the Coral Spas. "If people get to come back, why shouldn't dogs?"

"I don't know. I won't ask. You don't talk about such things."

I nodded. Here in Severny Spassk, death was always a private matter, something that happens behind a closed door and a tall *zabor*.

Mom once said it was all on purpose, to make sure people don't fade fast. If you give someone to the corals, they will return, at first even as a pretty corporeal entity. They just couldn't leave the village, never again. But then, as their remains submerge under more and more layers of dead polyps, their spirits begin to fade. It often happens by itself, but if they become aware of their own passing, the fading speeds up — and the more people know of that, the faster they fade, until nothing is left but a cold one, coming at night to wander around the village in search of anything warm.

"Think there's also cold ones in the city?" I asked. "Think Dasha ever seen one?"

"Here we go again..." Seryoga moaned. "Dasha this, Dasha that... Give me a break, man, *zadolbal*!"

***

"I heard that Severniy Spassk is weird," Dasha said. "Weird place with weird people. Is that true?"

"Am I weird?" I asked, finishing off the ice cream. It costed me a bit too much — I knew I'd have to walk back home, as the bus would be too expensive. But Dasha loved ice cream, so it was fine.

"You are," she nodded. "I mean, who even carves fish bones? And who buys that stuff? And all the weird things I hear about you people — you stay to yourselves, you don't let strangers in, and kids from your village don't make friends with any outsiders..."

"Well, I am here," I shrugged. "And you're here. So there's that."

She laughed and leaned into my shoulder. Her warm touch made my heart race.

"We had a kid from Severniy Spassk in my school," she said. "I think he was called Seryozha, Seryozha Korsikov... They went on a school trip this spring, and a drunken driver rammed into their bus. Seven kids died, I think..."

"It was six," I shook my head. "I know him. He was at first at the hospital, then his parents brought him home. They're now homeschooling him now, they don't trust the city people anymore."

"Don't trust the city people?" she giggled.

"Nope. You people are weird."

Dasha laughed and drew closer to me. She smelled of flowers and sweat, and still had some ice cream on her lips. It tasted good, sweet and milky.

***

"Seryozha dropped in yesterday, said the guys were playing ball," Mom said, handing me my oatmeal. "I thought you were with them. Did you run off to the city again?"

"Yes, Mom."

She frowned, her weary gray eyes full of anger and concern.

"You've been going there too often lately," she said. "I don't like it. Is it that girl you keep babbling about?"

"Yes, Mom. It's that girl. She's going to Turkey for a week soon, so I wanted to see Dasha more before..."

"The more you see her now, the worse it will hurt

when you break up," she said dryly. "Stop running off to the city so much... There's a lot of things to do around the house if you got so much time."

"Why should we break up?" I asked defiantly.

"Because a city girl won't want to live with you in some shabby *izba* here, and you cannot leave Severniy Spassk," she said, her voice colder than the great gray sea. "So give up on this *chepukha* and go play with your friends here."

"What if I move to her, though? Huh, Mom? What if I don't want to live in a shabby *izba* either?!"

"You can't leave," she repeated angrily. "If you do, you won't see Dad again, and you won't see me when I'm gone. And your children — you won't see them too after it's your turn to go, son!"

"So what?!" I screamed. "It's all the same here, every damn day, every damn year! Kids in the city go see movies, they go to Turkey, they have TV and eat ice-cream every day! Here, it's just work, hang around, sleep! There's nothing to do, Mom, I don't want this!"

"You stupid child," she hissed, standing up. "Let's go see you father — maybe, he can talk some sense into you."

In less than an hour, we were already in Ivan's small boat, with the man, clad in a fisherman's thick pullover, rowing away toward the small wooden church on top of the coral reef. It was built there many hundreds of years before and was rebuilt many times as the reef beneath it grew, feeding on the bodies of those given to the sea.

Father Grigori met us at the old, creaky pier. His eyes were the color of steel, and his hands holding the mooring rope looked like a raven's claws.

"Misha has lost his mind for a city girl, father," Mom said meekly. "I was hoping Oleg could talk some sense into him..."

"Outsiders only bring sorrows and plight," the priest nodded. "Keep your son away from that girl, she's nothing but the devil's temptation."

"Oh Lord, deliver us from evil," Mom whispered, crossing herself. "*Chur menya, chur!..*"

"Go pray for your son's good heart, kind woman," the

priest ordered her. "And you, Mikhail, follow me to the shrine. Your father's a man of reason, he will tell you how things are."

I followed the priest to the back of the church, to a small wooden door under a carved arch, all covered in dried salt. He opened it, and the cold wind from below pulled my hair, making me shiver.

"Go," the priest said. "Your father is waiting."

I made my way down the creaky old stairs to the grotto, where a small lamp hung over the dark waters. I could barely see the corals through it, the colorful blooming devouring bodies and bones.

"Dad," I said quietly. "Dad, are you here?"

"I am here, son," his voice, once deep and powerful, was now quiet like the whispers of autumnal leaves. I didn't even see him at first, the shadowy silhouette emerging from the waters to crawl toward me through the twilight. "I hear you stir trouble."

"I don't stir trouble, Dad," I sighed, crashing down on the wet wooden perch over the waters. "It's just that this girl, Dasha... She's special. I think I love her. And I want to be with her, that's it."

"You're just fifteen, son," he said, settling next to me. I couldn't make out his features no matter how hard I squinted, as if he was wearing a shadowy veil. God he was fading fast... Just a month ago, when we sat in this grotto carving together, he looked just the way he did before passing.

"So what? Can't I be in love?"

"Of course you can," he said with a sigh. "And it's good that you are. But in your age, things seem bigger than they are. What, think you want to leave, huh?"

"Why not, Dad?" I asked. "The city is so much cooler. And there's the bigger world out there, with the seas, and the mountains, and everything. Here, it's all gray nothing."

"Are me and Mom nothing?" he asked. "Are you nothing? You have no idea, son, how much it means to me to still be able to talk to you. To teach you the craft, to see you grow into a man, and watch over you while I still can. You think the city is worth all that? You take the good with the bad, that's how life is. And when you grow up, when you cool off, you'll see there's more good than bad here."

"But Dad, it's just all so… Empty. Why can't I hang out with her? Why do I have to spend all my life here? There's a whole world out there, why should I always stick to this place?"

"A man has to do what's right," Dad looked at the waters below. "This goes for you, but also for me. And as much as it would hurt me to see you go, you must make your own way… just remember, you always take the good and the bad, never only one, son. Now, get your knife. Let's carve."

***

Leaving the Coral Spas, I felt I had grown wings, so happy I was after the talk with Dad. My joy was premature, though, because the very next morning, I found that I couldn't leave my tiny room. Soon, Mom informed me that Father Grigori had spoken with Dad too and disagreed with his decision. He ordered Mom to keep me under lock until I give up my *blazh*, and she happily obliged.

I spent the next few days as a literal prisoner, stuck in my room 24/7, with Mom only opening the door to pass me food. I thought of making a run for it in those moments, but she made sure to stand in the doors, and I'd rather cut myself with my own carving knife than even push her.

One day, Seryoga snuck under my window, blocked off by a metal grate, and told me he had run into Dasha around the bus stop here. She came over to ask around what was up with me and say buy before Turkey, he said, and they caught tongues cause they had seen one another at school before.

"So why didn't you bring her here?!" I moaned. "Why, you fucking moron?!"

"I don't know," Seryoga said with this weird absent tone that was so untypical for him. "She said she thought I was dead, and it made me think… Like… I don't know, man. It just struck me, and it's still gnawing at me. Every day feels colder, so much colder now..."

"Get lost, you idiot!" I sobbed. "You ruined it, moron, how don't you get it?! She came for me, and now, she'll never come again!.."

He left indeed, quietly trudging away without cursing me back even once. Under different circumstances, that would have had me worried, but back then, I could only think of one thing: his betrayal.

Seryoga never showed up again, which made me all the more bitter, and as much as I pleaded with Mom to let me out, pledging I'd never even think of Dasha again, she didn't believe me. And rightfully so, cause I would have run off to the at the first chance, even though she wasn't there now. The good news was, Severniy Spassk wasn't there too, and I wanted to be as far from it as possible, just because of how sick and tired I had grown of my own small room.

I thought Mom would snap out of it in a few weeks, but I was wrong. In September, I didn't go to school; instead, I was released every now and then to study with Mom and whoever else she could scramble. Homeschooling was a big, big thing in Severniy Spassk, so there was no shortage of friends' parents who could teach me a thing or two. There was even a small school by the church — the one on the land, not on the reef — but Mom said it may be too early for me to go there, as I might still try running off.

Then, one cold autumn day, my imprisonment was over, as suddenly as it began.

"Your girl had left," Mom said. "Her dad got a placement in another city, and they moved. So don't go looking for her."

**

Seryoga had his own room, and a part of me really wanted to throw a brick there, just to make a point. But I had to throw a tiny pebble instead – making any noise at night would have been suicide.

At the third pebble, he squeezed his pale face against the glass, with the sleepy and scared look on his face that put a smile on mine. He squinted into the night, and I waved at him, signaling him to open the window.

"What the fuck are you doing?!" he whispered. "Why are you outside?! It's night, the cold ones are out!"

"Come. We're stealing the dynamite."

"What?!" his eyes grew as wide as two plates. "Are you crazy?"

"You said you know where your uncle keeps his explosives," I said coldly. "You ruined it for me and Dasha. You owe me. Take me to his stash or forget about our friendship."

"Mikhei, are you..." he gasped for air, trying to find the right words, then sighed and shook his head. "Okay. Fine. Whatever. Give me a minute."

In a few minutes, we were creeping together through the streets of the nightly Severniy Spassk, looking out for any movement around. It wasn't too dark – the burner on the rock over the village cast its crimson light upon its grim wooden houses and cold streets, and we saw the cold ones, the dark spider-like silhouettes crawling up to the flame.

Seryoga was quiet, untypically so. Even with the light from the burner, I couldn't really make out his face, for whatever reason, and couldn't tell what he may have been thinking. But I had bigger concerns.

Quietly, we made our way past the tall fences, wind tossing heaps of snow in my face. The shadows twirling around me felt alive, and I kept clenching the lightstick in my pocket. I didn't think it'd be enough to distract a cold one; truth was, nobody really knew if the flares worked for that either, but it was comforting to think I had something to defend myself with.

"Wait here, Mikhei," Seryoga whispered when we reached his uncle's house. "It'll be quick."

He disappeared for about ten minutes to remerge from the crimson twilight with several sticks of dynamite in his hands. They looked like in the movies, the long, red cylinders with cords on their end, all tied together.

"Thanks, man," I said, shoving the sticks in my backpack, next to the burners. "Wanna run away from here? With me?"

"What?!"

"Run away," I repeated. "Leave this damn place forever and ever. You want it?"

He hesitated for a bit, looking at the distant flame of the burner, covered by a veil of twirling shadows – the cold ones devouring the heat, which drew them like honey draws flies.

"Yes."

"Come with me, then."

He nodded and followed me into the night, through the empty streets full of anguish and fear, and to the old docks. As we made our way down the creaky old stairs to the pier, he spoke again, his voice faint and rustling.

"Where are we going? To the Spas?"

"To the Spas. We'll take the boat."

"Okay."

I didn't like that new voice of his. Something was off about Seryoga, and it freaked me out like hell, but then... He was a fellow prisoner here, not even given an option to go back to the town school. He may have ruined my chance to speak with Dasha, but he was still my best friend. And besides all that, I was just too scared to keep moving on my own.

I almost slipped when getting into Ivan's boat, rocked by the waves, but Seryoga caught my hand, helping me regain my balance. Did I feel how chilly his hands were even through my anorak, or was that a cruel joke that night played on me? I didn't want to know. I did light up a glowstick when we got on the boat, just to be safe, and the way he stared at it sent shivers down my spine.

It was a short, albeit arduous journey, and it left me completely out of breath, but we had to move. Up the wooden pier and stairs, slippery and covered in algae and seashells, to the small church, the grim church, which stood silent without a single light in its windows. Circle around it, walking quietly, to make sure Father Grigori wouldn't hear us. There it was — the heavy wooden door under the grim arch. It was never locked, to let those in the reef roam free (not that any lock would have held them back anyways), and I hurried toward it. Made it about half-way when I heard Seryoga's muffled scream.

The cold one approached me from the sea, its shadowy shape almost merging with the night, so I only saw it at the very last moment. Its long, distorted hands shot forth; I jolted back, but one of them still caught my leg. I screamed, falling flat on my back; it felt like my leg was caught in a bear trap, a devilishly cold one, and its frost was now making its way into my flesh like a thousand icy needles.

The first flare hissed, and a blood-red flame lit up at its tip — a flame that I shoved right in the cold one's face. It was gone in a heartbeat, its defiant light fading away in the darkness that made up this creature, and it made a weird, screeching noise, as if someone scratched glass.

It loved it, this wicked beast, it loved the light, and it loved the heat, and it wanted more.

"Get off him, *uebok*!" Seryoga rustled, kicking the cold one in its head. It paid little heed to him, raising its other arm, and he grabbed it with both hands, trying to keep it away from me.

I sobbed, feeling the stings of terrible, unfathomable cold crawling up my leg. I didn't really feel my ankle at that point, or the foot, for that matter, but I still had enough fight in me to light up another flare and toss it aside, hoping it would draw the creature away. And it did, surprisingly enough, as the next second, its freezing grip was gone.

Blinded by pain, I crawled back, tears running down my cheeks. Someone was shouting something to me, but I couldn't hear them, or even make out a single silhouette in the spiraling tornado of darkness before me. All I could was crawl, pulling my backpack behind me, and whimper in agony like a dying dog.

"Mikhei, run!" Dad shouted again. It was him who tossed the cold one off me, not the stupid flare — the damn thing was still hissing on the ground. "Run, get out, I'll hold it off!"

"Run, bro, we'll mess this *govnyuk* up!" Seryoga echoed, backing away from the brawl, closer and closer to the flare. "You show that bitch what's up, *Dyadya* Oleg!"

I couldn't stand up, I knew that without even trying, and even the thought of checking up on my leg was terrifying — I didn't want to see what the cold one's hand had done with it. It still hurt like hell, and as I crawled to the door, I couldn't hold back screams.

Into the cold corridor, and down the stairs, not as much crawling as just rolling down. I screamed in agony every time the hurt leg touched something, and the echoes of my agony mixed with the roar of the fight at the gate to produce a cacophony that made blood freeze in my veins.

"You'll be fine, Mikhei," I had no clue how Seroyga was there, he just popped out of the darkness, grabbed my hand, and helped me up, letting me rest my hand around his neck. I could feel the tickle of cold on my skin under the anorak. "You'll be fine, bro, just don't fade..."

"Down, man," I coughed. "Help me... down..."

"Sure, bro, sure... Mind lighting up another flare? it's dark as fuck in here..."

I lit up a flare for him, and he almost dropped me out of excitement. Can't remember how we made our way down, through the rumbling twilight and the screeches of the cold one. Hope Dad whooped its ass, real good... Too bad I didn't get to ask.

Down in the cavern, I could barely see the reef through the foaming waves in the pool. It was a stormy night, and the sea was raging beneath me, as if feeling what was about to happen.

I unzipped the backpack and pulled out the dynamite stick. Hesitated for a second, staring into the water below. For a second, I saw faces in the shapes the waves made, faces of those long gone. Some of them still retained their features, while others turned into blank masks, darkness staring at the world through their empty sockets. Those were the faces of the cold ones, I realized, the faces of those too far gone, mixed with those that were still like us. I even spotted a few familiar ones, even Dad was there, his gaze full of sadness...

I lit up the cord and tossed the stick down, then dropped on my back, frantically crawling away from the water.

"Seryoga!" I shouted. "Help! Get us out, now!!"

He looked at me and gasped, finally realizing what I had just done. Then, he rushed to me, grabbed my hands, and dragged me to the stairs. Every time my injured leg hit the stairs, sparks went off before my eyes, waves and waves of agony rolling over my body. I did feel the boom, though – the powerful eruption somewhere down, which made the entire world shiver. I even passed out, just for a second.

"Seryoga?!" I gasped out, looking around. "Dude, we did it... Just gotta get out of here now..."

The more I stared into the twilight, the better I realized I was alone on this rumbling rock, one on one with the old church collapsing on itself. Both Dad and the cold one were nowhere to be seen... And Seryoga was no more, too.

I sobbed, pushing my face into the snow. In a heartbeat, though, someone's claw-like hands grabbed my shoulders. A dark figure threw me on its back and hurried somewhere – to the pier, where the boat was, away from this crumbling structure.

"Foolish child," Father Grigori whispered. "Oh, what have you done..."

That was the last thing I remember of that night – his mournful whispers drowning in the waling wind, and the merciful darkness that rolled over me when he hurriedly tossed me into Ivan's old boat. Many things have happened since then; Severniy Spassk is no more, as the burial ground that held it together died in the blast. Mom and I now live in the city. She's got arthritis and can barely move, while I work 12-hour shifts at the factory just to pay for our tiny cold apartment. I've never met Dasha again, been single ever since we moved, in fact, and barely made any new friends.

I often think back to the day Dad said you have to do what's right. Wish I could I ask him if I had done right that day... But that chance was gone forever, as was the Coral Spas.

Phantoms
Gordon Linzner

Plodding 'neath the dark, foreboding skies
Hands jammed in pockets, shoulders hunched, lips tight
Alone – yet sensing far too many eyes
Neutral voices welcomed him this night
This graveyard was a place of dread and more
One tomb drew him close – he gave a groan
Mirrored in the crypt's reflective door,
Staring back, a dead man's face – his own!

In The Realm Of Shadow
Gina Easton

My daughter screams for me, blood-curdling, desperate cries. I plunge headlong into a vast darkness, frantically searching for her. The shadows are impenetrable, revealing only their mirror-image. My steps become heavier as I stumble forward. I feel like I'm wading through quicksand, sucked down through the ground. To Hell, perhaps. Perhaps it's where I belong.

Gilly shrieks again, her words barbed hooks that pierce my heart. "Mommy! Mommy, help!"

I open my mouth to yell, to tell her I am coming, I will save her. But the words freeze in my throat, ice-crystals, brittle and useless. In spite of my dread, the despair of inevitability, I blunder onwards. I stagger once, twice, before tumbling to the marshy, spongy earth. Gilly cries out a final time. Her voice is fainter, far away.

I know *he* has her. She is lost forever in the realm of shadow.

He has won. Again.

I thrashed awake, face streaked with tears. My heart pounded with wild fear.

Jack stirred beside me. A light sleeper, he is often disturbed by my nightmares. He sat up, and seeing my distress, wrapped me in a comforting embrace. "It's okay, honey," he whispered, stroking my hair. "Just a bad dream. Everything's alright."

But his words were a hollow lie. Nothing could make things 'alright'. My life was irrevocably disrupted the day I lost my daughter. Since Gilly was murdered. By a monster who hid in the depths of my past, feasting on the fears that suppurated, like a gangrenous wound, in the dark recesses of my soul.

My name is Nadine Saunders { nee Burnsfield}. You may have heard about my daughter's case twelve years ago. Gilly was seven years old when she 'disappeared.'

That was the term the police used, because they never discovered a body. Yet, I'm sure they believed, as I *knew*, that she was dead. The lead detective cautioned me not to give up hope, which wasn't an issue. I held out no hope from the beginning, Unlike the detective, I was fully aware of the fate that had befallen my daughter. She was taken by the Shadow-Man.

All those years ago, the Shadow-Man dwelt in a dumpster in an alley, not too far from our house. It was just Gilly and me. Her father was never in the picture. A fellow art student, he decided he was too young and carefree to be saddled with a family. We were twenty years old, with bright futures ahead.

Initially, I was ambivalent about motherhood. I had to reconcile putting my dream of being a commercial artist on hold, in favour of securing a steady-paying job, to support myself and the baby. To my surprise and relief, having a child to nurture and love was unimaginable joy. Gilly was a gift—bright, inquisitive, with a burning desire to uncover the wonders the world had to offer. I never dreamed that our happiness would be shattered, our lives decimated, by a monster from my childhood nightmares.

Gilly tried to warn me, did her utmost to make me understand, that the Shadow-Man was real. Too late, I realized how pernicious the menace was. Repressed memories finally surfaced, like a bloated corpse rises to the top of a lake. A traumatic incident from my childhood. A horrific murder, outside my bedroom window, perpetrated by the Shadow-Man.

The monster first appeared at night in my bedroom, lurking in the corner between the closet and window, directly across from where I slept. Because he blended in with the darkness, the only physical evidence of his presence was his eyes. Two red orbs, glowing with a fearful malevolence. Those eyes, glaring at me with such hatred, and the promise of unspeakable torment, terrified me so that I cried out for my mother. But of course, once she entered the room and flicked the light switch, we both saw that the corner was empty. Shadow-Man was clever. Infinitely cunning, he never allowed himself to be seen by anyone other than myself. Every bedtime was a horrifying prospect, for I never knew when I might awaken in the dead of night to find those blood-red eyes boring into my very soul, Shadow-Man sipping from my essence, savouring it like a fine wine.

The day the indigent man was discovered in the adjacent alleyway, beneath my bedroom window, I knew that he'd fallen victim to Shadow-Man. Abdomen slit to allow the escape of viscera, glistening organs, slick with blood and gore peeking out from their hidden cavern, eyes gouged out. I saw the man's body from my window, his horrified expression and gruesome visage traumatizing me so much that I willed myself to entomb it in the depths of my subconscious, a memory that could ultimately free my psyche, or break it.

And so I made myself forget everything to do with Shadow-Man and the vagrant's murder.

Fast-forward to my seven year-old daughter describing the *exact same* monster who lurked in the alleyway used by Gilly and her friends as a short-cut to school. I was utterly baffled when Gilly declared that her friends could not see this 'Shadow-Man'. He was only visible to her. Despite my unease, I assumed that my daughter's vivid imagination had conjured up this fiend. But I couldn't figure out *why*.

I was wrapped in a blanket of ignorance, a cocoon of denial, until, after Gilly's disappearance, I stood in the alleyway where she vanished, beside that sinister dumpster. I clutched Gilly's silver fairy pendant in shaking hands. It was the only tangible evidence my daughter left behind. All at once, the memories inundated me, a tsunami of terror, leaving me awash with so much pain and panic it hurt to draw breath. Followed by a grief so acute it pierced my heart like the sharpest blade. *Too late, too late*, echoed the mocking laugh of Shadow-Man in my brain. Too late to save my child.

For a long time after I was a shattered wreck. I wore my daughter's pendant as a constant reminder of my colossal failure to save her. I blamed myself for Gilly's death; guilt, a vicious rodent gnawing steadily at my soul, destroying it bite by bite. Only gradually did I emerge from a dense fog of grief, to find the world reflected back a dull, monochromatic grey. All colour, all vibrancy, leached from life. I wandered through a haze of existence. Suicide crossed my mind, but only fleetingly. I didn't deserve to end this pain. My path to atonement was to continue living, weighed down by misery. To be alone and lonely forever. The only way I could function was to distance myself from my emotions. I became an automaton, nothing more.

Then one day, Jack came into the art gallery where I worked, and my heart awoke. We had a whirlwind romance, married, and welcomed our twins, a boy and girl. I thought the worst was behind me.

***

The bedtime story was finished, and the twins snuggled in their beds. As I gazed at Leila it was hard to know whether my heart quickened in joy or pain. It was bittersweet, the way she reminded me so much of Gilly, not only in appearance, but personality.

She smiled impishly. "Mommy, can I be a princess when I grow up?" she asked.

I kissed the top of her curly tresses. "You can be anything you want, sweetheart."

She nodded, satisfied, then added, judiciously, "Or I might be a scientist. That'd be really cool, too."

I glanced at Cedric in the other bed. He was unusually quiet, even for him. His nature was totally different from that of his sibling, thoughtful, more reticent and introverted, in contrast to Leila's outgoing and exuberant character. Even at the age of six, he was serious, earnest beyond his years. Yet he sometimes displayed a dry sense of humour, and was quick-witted and intuitive.

"Is everything okay, honey?" I asked, sitting on the edge of his bed.

His hazel eyes were troubled. "There's something in the house next door."

My gaze travelled to the Reynolds' house, a property that had sat vacant for the last eight years, ever since Ron Reynolds killed his wife, Jeanine, in a domestic dispute.

As far as anyone was aware, the property remained in the possession of the Reynolds family, yet it hadn't been sold or rented. Not surprising. A lot of people were reluctant to occupy a "murder house". There were issues with the occasional vagrant or squatter, even an itinerant drug addict or two. However, increased police patrols, alerted by members of Neighbourhood Watch, put a stop to that.

I tried to ignore the house as much as possible. The tragedy of the Reynolds family struck too close to home. It seemed that the taint of murder and evil followed me, a rabid dog hell-bent on sinking its diseased fangs into me. Now, as I stared at the empty hulk sitting in the twilight, I shuddered involuntarily, reacting to my son's use of the word *something* rather than someone.

"What do you mean, Ced?" I asked uneasily. "What have you seen?"

His brow creased in a frown. "A monster."

My blood ran cold, but I endeavoured to remain calm. "A homeless person, maybe?" I asked hopefully.

He shook his head. "No. It was a monster. *Definitely*. It was looking out the window, watching me and Leila, here, in our room."

"Ah...what did it look like?"

His frown deepened. "I couldn't really tell, 'cause it was dark. The only thing I saw were its eyes. They were red and glowing."

Saliva turned to sawdust in my throat. I tried to swallow the fear rising like noxious bile.

"When did you see him?" I whispered.

"Last night." Ced's eyes searched my face anxiously. He could tell that this information had shaken my composure. "Just two eyes, Mommy. But I was scared."

I nodded, not trusting myself enough to speak.

"It *had* to be a monster, right, Mommy? Because of its red eyes," Leila said insistently.

"Of course it was," her brother replied, in a tone that left no room for doubt.

They both looked at me, waiting for me to say something, offer some reassuring 'Mommy-speak'. I hated to let them down, but I couldn't pretend. I knew the

Shadow-Man, and that intimate familiarity had already cost me too much.

"How come you're only telling me now?" I asked my son, managing as normal a tone as I was able.

Cedric's bottom lip trembled and his eyes filled with tears. "*He* said not to tell you," he whispered miserably. "Otherwise," his gaze darted to his sister, "otherwise...he said...he would...*eat* Leila."

Leila gasped and leaped out of bed to throw herself in my lap. "Don't let him, Mommy. "Don't let the monster eat me."

I held my daughter tightly, soothing her, stroking her hair, until her terrified weeping calmed. I took her small face, blotchy and pinched from her tears, in my hands. I said firmly, looking into her eyes, "*No monster* is going to eat you." I included Cedric in my glance. "*Either* of you. Ced, that was very brave of you to tell me. Only, how did the monster speak to you?"

My son shrugged. "Dunno. I just heard a whisper in my head. His voice was really creepy. He said grown-ups don't believe in monsters, anyway."

Well, this was one grown-up who did. Shadow-Man knew it, just as he knew my child would not be able to keep such a disturbing secret to himself. How awful, to place this horrible burden on my son. The monster was counting on my old fear of him, plus the trauma and grief of Gilly's death, to paralyze me and render me helpless to protect my children

But that would not happen. I was no longer an eight year old girl cowering under the blankets. I wasn't helpless. My fear did not control me. In its place was a growing outrage that this fiend had the gall to try to rip my life apart once again. I didn't yet know how, but I would find a way to save my children, to protect them from this horror. No other option was acceptable.

After the twins were settled, I went downstairs and out the door of the kitchen, to stand in our backyard. Twilight had deepened to full darkness. I gazed at the Reynolds' house, struck by how forlorn it seemed. It had that air of neglect, bereft as only an abandoned house could be, yet I sensed something astir within its walls. A sinister undercurrent, spawned by the evil entity that now occupied the dark recesses of the structure. The monster, whipping up dust motes with its covert, stealthy movements. Shadow-Man, amorphous, substance-less, yet all too real, with burning eyes to strike terror into the most stalwart heart. Shadow-Man was anti-matter, composed of obsidian particles, black grains of sand, held together by the sheer force of evil.

Though he refused to show himself tonight, I knew he was aware of me, as I observed his new dwelling.

He was biding his time.

***

How did I begin to tell Jack? All he knew of Gilly's tragedy was what I'd told him, that my daughter had been abducted and killed by person{s }unknown. No mention of monsters made of shadows, of glowing, demonic eyes, of evil that existed beyond this earthly realm. I believed, correctly or not, that anyone who'd never felt the taint of corruption, could possibly accept my tale as the truth. As time went on and my relationship with Jack deepened, it seemed imperative that I guard my secret. Simply put, I was afraid, of losing Jack, of being alone again, of the inevitable black nights ahead.

All that long night I battled with my thoughts. Even if, by some miracle, Jack were to believe my past encounters with Shadow-Man, he wouldn't have a clue how to combat an evil of this magnitude. Jack was *normal*. Normal people didn't know how to vanquish monsters. My childhood and adult experiences were too strange, too incomprehensible to someone like my husband. He'd gone through childhood believing in the innate goodness of the world, never suspecting the vileness that lurked just beyond the perimeters of this reality. A vileness that sometimes managed to infiltrate those boundaries, and threaten the lives, and very sanity, of mere mortals.

This battle with evil was mine, alone. I needed to face it, not only for the sake of my children, but to conquer the fear that had plagued me all my life, casting a blight on my childhood. Fear was a wraith that stalked me, and Shadow-Man, its embodiment. Being a parent once more had heightened that fear into a nagging terror that lurked in my heart. The loss of a child was the worst nightmare a parent could endure. Losing *three* children to the same fiend was unimaginable. I was fighting not only for my children's lives, but for the preservation of my soul.

All in all, the stakes were as high as they could be.

The next day, I got the twins ready for school, drove them to their first-grade class, made one stop on the way home, called in sick at the art gallery. Then I waited. Waited for Jack to leave for work. Waited to be alone so I could think.

And then, I went to the Reynolds' house.

I didn't have to scale the fence, as there was a gate between our two houses. I didn't know if the back door was locked, but I *did* know I would have no trouble gaining entry. Sure enough, the doorknob turned easily and I walked into the Reynolds' abandoned kitchen. A distinctly unpleasant smell greeted me; a pungent combination of mold and rodent droppings. The floor was intact, if worn and scuffed in places. Layers of dust covered every surface, but did not obscure the myriad cobwebs peeking out from corners, suspended from ceiling and light fixtures. Epitome of a haunted house, it was decked out in its best Halloween finery. The atmosphere was heavy and brooding. The building had soaked up the negative energy generated by the abuse and murder that had taken place within its confines. Over the years that energy had twisted and turned upon itself, mutating into a decaying putrefaction that had seeped into the very bones of the house.

Now, Shadow-Man had added to that roiling, diseased energy, creating a vileness so potent I could almost taste it.

My stomach began to churn and I fought the queasy sensation. I could not afford any distractions, any attempts by my body to betray me. I still didn't have a concrete plan. I knew I had to confront the monster and defeat him once and for all, to stop his relentless stalking. Otherwise, I would live the rest of my life in abject fear, always waiting for him to reappear, to threaten me and my family. It wouldn't matter how many times we moved, or where, Shadow-Man would hunt us down. A cold, prickly sweat broke out over my body as I contemplated this scenario, and the bleakness of such a future.

I continued my progress through the house. The family-room was dark and silent, the windows grimy enough to act as a barrier to any natural light. Misshapen lumps that might have been furniture could just as easily turn out to be malignant imps ready to jump at me. I decided to bypass the room. Shadow-Man wasn't there. He was upstairs, waiting for me.

In true haunted house fashion, the steps creaked as I ascended the staircase. They echoed eerily in the silence, which pressed on me, laden with hostility and menace. This house, with its darkness, its sordid history, was Shadow-Man's ally. A strong feeling of loneliness came over me as I realized that no human being could help me now. If I failed, if I didn't make it out of this house alive, no-one would find my body, at least not for a long time. Perhaps never. I had known stark solitude before, when the pain of my thoughts lanced through my entire being, when every moment promised only more grief and sorrow. Now, that old abyss of anguish threatened to crack open beneath me, and drag me down to its unforgiving maw.

I murmured Gilly's name, like a mantra, to focus my thoughts. As I touched the silver fairy pendant around my neck, the acute misery subsided, leaving a calm and lucid reassurance. I conjured up Gilly's image, and felt my heart suffused with her sweet essence, a nectar more precious than gold or jewels. Tears of gratitude sprang to my eyes. My daughter might have been brutally wrenched from this existence, from me, but somehow, she lived inside my heart, my soul.

With new-found hope and courage, I forged up the stairs. Reaching the landing, I paused to orient myself. There were three bedrooms and a bathroom. I located the room that Shadow-Man occupied when he spied on the twins, and headed towards it. It was darker in the upstairs rooms. Even though the doors were opened, my vision could not penetrate the interior gloom. Shadow-Man could be anywhere. But he was everywhere, of that I was certain.

I could have brought a flashlight, or my cell phone, but somehow I intuited that darkness was to be a crucial component of this encounter. Part of the goal of defeating the monster was to conquer my terror of the dark. Steeling myself for whatever might ensue, I entered the bedroom.

It was cold in there, a cold that clutched at me with icy fingers as it tickled its way into my bones. Some people assume, I guess because of evil's association with the devil and hell, that evil burns hot. Evil is cold and it will freeze your heart if you let it. I bet that Hell itself is colder than an Arctic tundra, more chilling than the darkest depths of the ocean. Still holding my daughter's pendant, I visualized a warm shield around my heart, the protective flames repelling the frigid tendrils of evil. A few moments passed, and then I became aware of an abatement of the cold. My heart beat steady and strong. I moved forward into the room, feet scuffing through the dust like it was sand.

I gazed around the room, but couldn't make out any features. The darkness was uniform. Unsure of my next move, I simply stood still, waiting. It wasn't long before I was aware of a subtle shift in the atmosphere, an almost intangible re-arranging of molecules of darkness. A slight rustling noise was followed by a swirling eddy of shadows.

Then the glowing red eyes sent a shiver of dread into my core, pinning me to the spot. I was catapulted back to my eight year-old self, trembling in a corner of my bed, sure the terrible monster would devour me to my core. Those eyes, filled to the brim with malice and oily glee, drew me toward their wicked depths. I knew that if I could not look away or blink, I would be engulfed by a vileness that would make my past miseries shrivel to a pale husk in comparison with this new level of heightened suffering.

Mustering my will-power, I tried to blink. I couldn't. My eyelids were frozen open. In rising panic I did the only thing that came to mind. I bit down on my tongue, hard enough to cause blistering pain and tears to spring to my eyes. But my ploy was successful. That action and the ensuing pain broke the monster's hypnotic spell and I tore my gaze away, forcing myself to look at a spot higher up along the wall behind the demonic orbs.

A sardonic chuckle echoed in my mind. The fiend knew what I had done, but seemed nonchalant about it, like he was merely toying with me, which was probably the case. It suddenly occurred to me how great a mismatch this was. I would need every ounce of strength, both physical and spiritual, to beat Shadow-Man, while he could amuse himself playing games with me until I collapsed from exhaustion. It was David and Goliath all over again, only without the sling-shot. *My* secret weapon was a good deal less reliable than that.

I stood my ground, waiting for the next cue from my nemesis. My hand slipped into my jacket pocket and found the small vial of holy water I'd picked up from Saint Dorothy's Church that morning. I'd sprinkled some on the fairy pendant, saving the rest for when I would need it. Maybe it was a lame idea. Before Gilly's death I hadn't thought much about God. After my memories of the monster surfaced, I reasoned that if such evil existed, then surely good, in the form of a benevolent supreme Being, must as well. But that was really the extent of it. I couldn't accept that a God who was loving would allow a heinous tragedy like Gilly's to occur. Yet, as I stood in this awful house with its tainted energy, I felt that God was the only one upon whom I could rely if I were to emerge unscathed from this ordeal, hence the holy water. It might prove a desperate and futile measure, but I was nothing, if not desperate, to end this ordeal once and for all.

I didn't need to look at those blood-red eyes to know where the fiend was. Shadow-Man seemed to fill the entire room, blotting everything else out. It was just me and this entity.

"Why won't you show yourself to me?" My voice echoed hollowly off the walls of the room.

Another chuckle. *I am shadow*, the voice whispered in

my head. *But you, Nadine, can see me, if you really desire to.*

A tingle of dread rushed down my spine. Shadow-Man knew my name.

I couldn't fight a monster that I couldn't see. The red orbs had changed position to the left of me. I focused my gaze on that spot, careful to avoid a direct look at those baleful eyes. The fiend was right. As my gaze intensified, I discerned a shape that was separate from the general darkness, a rough silhouette of a person. It wasn't lighter, simply a different *shade* of black. Shadow-Man was just as I remembered from my childhood.

All the anguish I'd suffered before, rose up from that dark cubbyhole in my heart, and I cried out, "Why can't you leave me alone? Why have you come to torment me again?"

There was a silence before the response came. *You know why. I told you all those years ago. Sadly, you chose to forget. But now there will be a reckoning, a reclaiming.*

"I don't understand what you mean!" I sobbed, rage and fear battling for control of me.

The monster inched closer, the glowing eyes boring into me.

"No!" I screamed as the rage finally won out. "You will not take my children." I whipped out the vial of holy water and hurled its contents at him.

Shadow-Man laughed again. *An ineffectual ploy. In order for that to work, your faith in God must be more powerful than your fear of me. And we both know that isn't true. Still, after all these years, you persist in your denial. It isn't your children I want, Nadine. It's you. It has always been you.*

Then the fiend rushed at me and I felt myself engulfed in a darkness as thick and greasy as tar, and as foul-smelling, as one by one, my senses were extinguished.

***

I awoke to find myself in an unfamiliar room, hooked up to some kind of monitor that beeped at regular intervals. An intravenous tube was attached to my left arm. Jack was sitting in a chair beside my bed.

"Nadine! Thank God, you're awake." His face was etched with concern as he bent over me.

"What happened?" I asked weakly.

Jack shook his head. "We don't know for sure. I came home to find you lying unconscious on the kitchen floor. An ambulance brought you here. The doctor said your heart beat was erratic so they hooked you up to a cardiac monitor. He also said you were seriously dehydrated. That's why you have the IV. But they're not sure why you collapsed.

"How do you feel, honey?"

How *did* I feel? A simple enough question, yet I had no ready answer. In a way, I felt like I wasn't actually *there*. I mean, I understood that I was in hospital, and Jack was by my side, but I didn't *feel* anything in particular. There was a disconnection between my body and the rest of me. Physically, I was aware of my bodily functions, my heartbeat, breathing, swallowing. I could move all my limbs. But *inside* there was an emptiness, a void where my emotions used to reside.

I looked at my husband, waiting for the familiar rush of tenderness and love to envelop me. It didn't happen. I *ought* to feel love for this man, and experience his love for me. Yet none of that was present. I wasn't upset by this, not in the least disturbed by this unusual phenomenon. Perhaps the doctors would have an explanation for what had happened to me.

But I thought not. For I remembered what occurred in the Reynolds' house just before I blacked out.

I was discharged from the hospital the next day. The doctors were puzzled by my 'episode', having found no physiological reason for my erratic heartbeat {which resolved spontaneously}. They spoke about a possible autonomic nervous system anomaly having triggered an episode of syncope, which would explain the blacking-out. Otherwise, I was pronounced a 'healthy young woman' with the proviso that I follow up any concerns with my family doctor.

Jack was relieved, I could see that, and so happy to be

taking me home. As for me....well, I felt nothing. Even the thought of reuniting with my children gave me no joy. The only remnant of my former self lay in my maternal instinct. A tiny kernel of that remained, unsullied by the fiend's corruption. And I was determined to hold onto it for as long as I could.

***

You were spawned from darkness. And to darkness you shall return.

Shadow-Man's words ripped through me, shredding a hole in my psyche, tearing my soul apart. I felt his inky filth, the creeping sludge of his essence infiltrate every pore of my being.

It is time for you to fulfill your destiny, to continue the work I have begun. Time for us to finally be together, my daughter, my child.

I wanted to scream and thrash with all my strength, to rage against the insanity of those words. But I was a petrified statue, unable to move a muscle. And the more Shadow-Man's corruption poured into me, the more I recognized the truth of his words. The putrid stench of evil began to seem like the sweetest aroma ever, a headiness as of a thousand orchids blooming at once. My body began to tingle pleasantly. I giggled, even though a tiny portion of my consciousness recognized the *wrongness*. I was mutating, becoming the entity I was meant to be. Understanding dawned on me. My childhood fears had been totally unfounded. All those times I thought Shadow-Man's eyes were filled with malice, it was actually *love* reflected in them. He was watching over me, keeping me *safe* throughout my youth. Secure in this revelation, I surrendered to the darkness, to my father.

***

Now I can do one last thing before that tiny window of light slams shut in my soul forever. I vowed to protect my children from the monster, so I will. I will protect them from *me*. I will leave my family, go far away, never to return. My children and husband will grieve, but they will survive, and eventually move on with their lives. I will journey with my father, to the ends of the earth and back, and we will wreak havoc and misery wherever we go. It is what we do.

Only it won't be just the two of us. My father made me a promise.

I always knew I would be reunited with Gilly.

Lakefront Property
Keith LaFountaine

1.

I hear the first scream while buying watery gas station coffee. It's a shrill thing, sharp and thick, more of a wrenched gasp than a shriek. But it affects me, nonetheless. I cringe by the coffee urns, hissing as black liquid burns my hand, and glance around. My heart climbs into my throat like a needy house cat.

It takes me a moment to realize that nobody else hears it. There is a man in a yellow hardhat by the coolers, choosing between Dr. Pepper and Coke; there is an old woman raising a shaking finger and jabbing it toward one of the many scratch-offs behind the register; there is a kid, no older than fifteen, grabbing a warm pizza slice. But they all go about their business.

The skin on the back of my hand turns a cherry hue in a matter of seconds. I wipe it along the side of my pants, shiver, and resume pouring my coffee.

When I bring it up to the register, I search the cashier's face for any hint of recognition. He looks at me evenly.

"That all?" he asks in a tired drawl.

"Sure," I say, nodding. Then, clearing my throat, "Yeah."

2.

Forty-two minutes later, I sit in stalled traffic down on Pine Street. Construction workers stand around and stare at an open hole in the pavement. I drum my hand on the wheel. Dire Straits is on the radio, and I absentmindedly sing along, thankful I chose to fill my tank after getting coffee.

A chill caresses my cheek, and then a scream – full throated and shrieking, like a revving engine lacking a muffler – bursts in my ear. I jerk to the left, accidentally taking the wheel with me. Thankfully, my foot is on the brakes, so all I do is turn my tires.

I sit very still. The hairs on my arm are raised, and goosebumps rise like a medieval pox. The scream fades, giving way to chattering machinery and honking horns. But I *feel* it, there in my ear, as if someone has died in my passenger's seat. And not just died but has been brutally mangled. As if I'll turn and see viscera splashing the dashboard and shining bone sticking out of the vents and blood dripping through the partially cracked window.

That chill stays with me, even as the sun rises, and when I escape the traffic and get to work, I sprint to the bathroom where I promptly vomit the watery coffee into the closest toilet.

3.

My therapist, a man named Jess, is kind enough, but I know his *disbelieving* face. He employs it now, donning the wrinkled lips and the tired eyes like they're Halloween accoutrements, something to round out a scary costume. He lets his notepad lilt in his lap, and he crosses his legs, leaning his cheek on steepled fingers.

"Screams?" he asks.

I pick at my fingernails, realize I'm doing it, and stop, covering one hand with the other. My palms are always sweaty, but right now they feel as if they're birthing rivers.

"I know how it sounds," I say.

He shrugs. "How's work going? The promotion?"

I chew on my bottom lip. I think about all the blue sheets in my office. All the carefully planned out lines on X and Y and Z axes.

"It's fine," I say, even though the lie tastes rancid in my throat. "It's slow-going. I'm working on a new building downtown. Something right on the water."

Jess gives an appreciable nod and adjusts his posture, securing the notepad against one of his legs.

"What do you think the screams sound like?" he asks. "Is it someone you know?"

I think about the question for a while, and he gives me

space to do so. That's one of the reasons I like him; he's thoughtful. Or maybe he's just letting me eat up a hundred-eighty seconds of my fifty-minute hour.

"A few years ago, I had a dream about my friend Shannon," I say, choosing my words like fancy candies from a display. Testing each one, trying out how it feels in my mouth, before deciding to emit it. "In the dream, it was the middle of the night. I think one or two in the morning. I don't remember waking up -- in the dream, I mean – but I sat up in bed. All the lights were off, and I looked over at my bedroom door, and I realized it was open. No...I realized it was open *and* that someone was standing out there. Just an amorphous shadow. There was no moonlight, no headlights from the parking lot. Just...a void. And I opened my mouth to ask what she wanted for dinner, but before I could, she smiled. And I couldn't see anything other than that smile. Her teeth were bright white, like they'd been bleached far beyond what was safe. And the rest of her face was still bathed in shadow. The smile grew wider, and...I thought I heard flesh tearing. Like, her cheeks. I heard it with such clarity."

I pause. My pants are now soaked with sweat. I wipe them haphazardly along the material, but that only serves to spread the moisture around.

"Did you wake up then?"

I nod. "I heard something jingling, in the dream. I thought it was a neighbor playing marimbas. But I woke up, and I answered the phone."

"Who was on the other line?" Jess asked.

I pick at my nails again. Realize. Stop. "Her boyfriend, Mark, telling me she was dead."

4.

After putting the chicken in the oven and letting out a long sigh, I pull my corkscrew from the "everything" drawer (don't lie; you have one, too) and unearth my corkscrew. As I drive the sharp, silver tip into the wood, my phone begins to buzz. I huff, hold the corkscrew and the bottle with one hand, and deftly answer the call, putting it on speakerphone with the other.

"Hello?" I ask.

"Hey, Liv. It's Paul." My boss. Of course.

"Hey, Paul," I say. I twist the corkscrew and watch its arms raise out to each side like a bugged-out videogame character.

"I just got off the phone with the mayor," he says. "Guy wants to help us, but protestors are digging up every piece of arcane zoning law they can. They now want to see if they can submit for the plot of land to be a *place of historical significance* because, apparently, Ethan Allen stood there back in 1700-who-the-fuck-knows."

"Uh huh," I say, yanking the cork out. I think about grabbing a glass but press the bottle's rounded edges to my lips instead. "What's that mean?"

"For you? Nothing beyond another delay. But I may pull you into some of these meetings. We gotta smooth things out with these protestors. God forbid a zoning lawyer decides to look into stuff for them pro bono."

"Well, I've got chicken in the stove. Can we chat about this tomorrow?"

"Sure," Paul says.

We share some small talk about Vermont autumns, and then I hang up. The chicken still has five minutes, so I take another pull of wine. I'm about to wander into the living room when my phone buzzes again. I don't even look at it; I slide the circular icon across and put it on speaker.

"Hello?"

Silence.

I put the wine bottle down and pick up the phone, glancing at its screen. **UNKNOWN** adorns the top of the call in capital letters.

Great.

Is this one of those scam calls? I'd read a story a few days prior that mentioned a new tactic. They'd get you to answer your phone and—

A horrendous, wailing scream bursts through the phone's speaker. I can hear vocal cords being shredded in the sound, as if some masked killer with a massive carving knife is hacking away at the tender organ. But it doesn't blunt the sound; if anything, it adds texture to it. I hear the careening horror, the fear, the certainty of death. It's all there in that one, unending sound.

I drop my phone out of sheer instinct. It *cracks* on the floor in such a way that I can tell I've shattered the screen. When the device hits the tile, the scream cuts out.

My legs feel like gelatin. I grip the edge of the counter to stop myself from falling – and, potentially, cracking something. Nausea climbs in my throat once more, and I wonder if I'm going to paint my kitchen a similar version of what painted my work's toilet bowl that morning. But everything stays down, thank God. The goosebumps are back, though, and they aren't receding. Worse yet, I taste electricity in the air. My hair crackles with static.

I kneel and pick the phone up. The screen is indeed shattered, but as I stare at it, I lose all interest in the chicken that's cooking – the chicken I spent the better part of twenty minutes preparing and seasoning.

Because the savage snarl along the glass is shaped in a wide, unyielding grin, spreading from the base toward each side.

5.

Four protestors stand outside our building with posterboard signs. Each one has a cruel message about us written along its face.

MURDERERS, shouts one.

FASCISTS, yells another.

But it's the third that catches my eye as I hold my cheap coffee in one hand and my car keys in the other.

MAY YOU HEAR THEIR SCREAMS, it reads.

A chill wraps around me like an old leather jacket, and I shrug it off, scanning my keycard and entering the building.

6.

Paul is on the phone with the mayor for most of the morning. I hear snippets of their conversation. Something about the election and local sympathies toward the homeless camps around the city. And it's true – the protestors are growing by the day. I've checked Reddit a time or two, half-expecting to see my face plastered on the front page of r/Burlington. Thankfully, no dice on that front. But there is no shortage of vitriol aimed our way. We went from obscurity to notoriety in just one week. It's no wonder to me that my predecessor drove himself off a bridge after having the camp cleared out.

I finish my coffee and dump it in the trash can beside my desk.

7.

The bath is comfortable, especially after a long day of pushing paper and grinding my teeth. It's even better with some wine, an edible, and candles. I think about playing music, or maybe about continuing that audiobook I bought two months ago, but decide against both options, opting for pure, blissful silence.

The warm water laps around my kneecaps, and I feel the warmth sinking into my bones, caressing me, inviting me deeper, and I follow that siren song with my eyes closed and the smell of lavender filling the bathroom.

When I open my eyes, it's pitch black. The candles have been snuffed out. I wonder, only for a moment, if I've forgotten to buy new ones. But no, I recall them being full of wax. They weren't brand-new, but they were new enough. And that's when I realize the water is cold. Freezing, in fact, and it's *sticking* to me. Staining me.

My teeth chatter, and I go to leave the tub – to scramble out of it, in fact – only to hear the clink of a chain. I tug again, and I feel the weight of a collar around my neck. My fingers brush against the looping metal coils attached to a gapless circlet, and that chain leads down the drain.

It starts to pull, the chain. Pull me deeper. Pull me toward the dark, the wet, the cold, the filmy feeling of it all. I plant my feet against the tub's front, and I pull at the chain, but it rips my palms open, and they weep blood.

The collar around my neck tightens, and the chain continues to methodically *clink, clink, clink* as each loop clacks against the drain and descends into its depths.

Nothing is going to save me, I realize. I look around the bathroom wildly, and that's when I see an amorphous shadow standing in the open doorway.

I try to open my mouth, to say her name, but all that comes out is a silent wheeze, a puff of squeezed air, clenched in the savage collar, saved for later. My body is slipping deeper now. My foot is inside the drain and it's descending, as if that small hole has widened to allow me through. The liquid is cold, and it adheres to my body like glue. Tears, wet and hot, slide down my cheeks. I open my mouth again, but the sludge slips in, and I recognize the coppery tang of it.

Blood.

The shadow brightens as too-white teeth flash. The smile widens until it bites into both cheeks, and somehow it spreads further. I hear flesh ripping, tendons wheezing. And beneath all that, I hear her screaming.

Then, I am under the water, my thigh disappearing down the drain, the plumbing hungrily devouring me. The collar chokes me of all oxygen, and I give what fight I have, wrenching and writhing and gasping, and I see that horrible smile in the doorway. I hear her—

I jerk upright in the tub, water sloshing over the side and splashing along the tile floor, spluttering.

I'd fallen asleep.

I hack and cough. The candles shine bright, as they did when I closed my eyes. And the doorway is empty. But the tub's water is so very, very cold.

8.

Paul calls me in the morning. I paw at my phone and sleepily answer. "Yeah?"

"We're in the clear," he says. "Mayor's office bulldozed those nonsense *historical landmark* claims. We'll be free to break ground come Monday morning."

I don't have it in my heart to celebrate the news, so I

just nod and say, "Good to hear. Thanks."

"Strap in your seatbelt," he says. I can hear the grin in his voice. "Big things are coming your way."

Strap in your seatbelt.

Liv, give me the keys.

"Sure," I say. He tries to make small talk. I give him one-word answers. We hang up. I hold the phone in my hands.

Give me your keys, Liv. I'm serious.

I look to my left. My closet door is open. Did I—

The scream is so powerful I am forced to my right, as if a hurricane is shouldering through the doorway. The sound is high-pitched; it claws at my eardrums, and it burrows into my brain like a Lovecraftian worm. Shivers wrack me, as does nausea, and I spill off the side of the bed as the closet door slams against the drywall, hard enough to leave a dent. The window behind me crackles, and when I turn to look at it I see streaking lines spreading out from the center.

I curl up into a ball on the floor and hold my hands to my ears. Tears spring in my eyes, and saliva pools from my mouth into the carpet.

When I pull my hands away, some interminable time later, the scream has ended. But the dent in my wall is still there. And the cracks remain.

9.

We may have won the legal battle, but protesters are still picketing the site. If anything, they've only grown. The mayor's progressive challenger – a young City Council member with a swath of blond hair and piercing, blue-green eyes, holds a megaphone and shouts into it. His voice crackles across the crowd, and every so often they cheer and lift their posterboard signs.

I shiver and cross my arms. It's eighty degrees in Burlington today, and the sun is shining, but I can feel my body temperature falling off a cliff.

Mr. Young Upstart catches a glimpse of me and points. The crowd shifts focus. I brace myself for their fury. For their unrepentant righteousness. But they do something much worse.

They smile.

All of them.

The smiles spread wide, so wide that I worry I'll soon hear—

Screams echo across the lake, glancing off the water, breaking the sound barrier, filling the sky. Birds take flight and flap their wings, but I can't hear them. All I can hear is wrenching vocal cords and strained phlegm and pure horror.

Liv, give me-

LIV—

Screeching metal. Burning tires. The smell of smoke. Waking up while we're midflight. And Shannon's voice breaking as she was thrown around the car's interior, glass ripping her cheeks, her head smashing against the windshield, leaving a crimson smear.

Echoing screams, and then nothing at all, until the car hit the water.

And now, those screams careen over the lake, at me.

"Can't you hear that?" I bellowed to them. "Can't you hear her?" Tears hang in my eyes.

"Huh," Mr. Young Upstart says into his loudspeaker. "Maybe she has a heart after all."

I turn away, sprint to my car, and they watch me go before turning back to the topic at hand. But I hear someone laughing, amidst it all.

I don't think it was Mr. Young Upstart, and I don't think it was in the crowd.

10.

On Monday, the protesters are arrested. Bulldozers are brought in. Machinery beeps as it backs up, and men in neon vests and orange hardhats shout orders at other men in neon vests and orange hardhats.

I stand nearby, my back to the lake. Paul is beside me. We look out as bulldozers turn over dry dirt and reveal deep, rich soil.

"I don't know what's got them all hot and bothered," Paul says, nodding toward the last of the protesters, who are being ushered away in handcuffs. "Not like hobos took care of things. Hell, most of 'em were pissin' in the lake and shitting in the grass."

I don't answer. I look to my right, maybe out of instinct, maybe out of some sixth sense I've developed over the years.

Standing there, over by the forest, amidst bramble and pine needles, is a shadow. I squint, trying to see more, but all I discern is that the skin on one hand is pale blue. Water beads at the end of the fingertips and spills to the soil.

Someone screams. I've become accustomed to the sound in an odd way, and as much as it shocks me, I don't turn toward it. I look at this shadow as thoughts race through my mind.

It can't be.

It can't...

"Liv!" Paul shouts.

But it's too late. I feel the crash of machinery against my chest – a dirt-raked claw that jerks to the right. It flings my body back toward the lake.

I break through the surface.

Water rushes into my mouth, choking me, slipping into my lungs. The claw knocked what air I had out, and now I am sinking into the dark depths, writhing, my feet, my arms, my hands. The light above grows dimmer, even as I reach for it, even as I sink into the darkness.

She's waiting for me there. That's what I think as my body spasms and my lungs desperately contract, sucking for air that isn't there.

She's down there, still in the car.

And I think, when I get there, she'll smile.

Whispers and Shadows
Ivy B

The shivering cold runs through my back;
Desperate for even a weak flame of a candle,
The yearning for warmth is progressing, undeniable,
The whispers get louder with every step forward.
Fear and exhaustion consume me, yet I'm intoxicated
Drowning in this swamp of lethal symphony,
– Like a pirate falling into a trap, woven with a
 Siren's melody.
Freezing, with every breath I exhale
Bits of my life come out of me
Spiraling into this grey mist;
The shadows I see in the corner of my eyes
– like predators waiting to ambush their prey.
And someday the last pieces of me will escape,
The last drop of me will dissipate,
For the shadows to feast upon them.

I'm New Here Myself
Matt Betts

 A chupacabra
 Big city bright lights shining down
 Where are all the goats?
 I'm hungry and bored out here
 My kingdom for some cattle

Barry's Gate
Ann O'Mara Heyward

They had never gotten along, you might say.

When Sarah bought the house, it hadn't occurred to her to check out the next-door neighbors first. There was just one house on either side of hers; hers was set back two hundred feet from the street on a bowling-alley lot adjoining a park in the rear. On her left as she faced the street were Kristin and Dave Fowler; on her right, although she didn't know his name yet, was Barry Finnegan. She had liked Kristin and Dave from the beginning. Several weeks went by before she met Barry.

Because her house was set so far back from the street, and Barry's lot was smaller, his back yard was next to her front yard and enclosed by a six-foot-high stockade fence. At the rear of his lot, a single gate opened onto a heap of fallen branches, a pile of leaves and grass clippings, and an aluminum fishing boat turned upside down. The mess annoyed Sarah, who had to look at it from her own side yard, but since it was on his property there was little she could do about it.

It was October when she and Barry finally met. If you could call it that, she thought later. She spent that day raking leaves and planting bulbs that would bloom next spring. She stood on her lawn in the gathering dusk, knuckling the small of her back, twinging from the hours of yard work. The peace was shattered by a desperate squealing, an animal in pain. From next door on the right, behind the fence.

"There, you son of a bitch," a man's voice said, followed by what sounded like bone crunching. The terrible squealing stopped. Sarah dropped her rake and walked over to the fence line next to her driveway. She was five-six; the fence was higher than her head. She could not see into the yard.

"What the hell was that?" she asked. Something came sailing over the fence and landed with a limp plop at her feet. In the waning daylight, she could not see what it was at first and squatted down to look. She rocked back on her heels, and nearly fell on her ass in her own driveway. It was a dead rabbit, its head crushed and one leg terribly mangled. The bastard had caught it in a leg-hold trap, then smashed its skull. "You *asshole,*" she yelled, enraged. Behind the fence, she heard laughter, then heard the back door to the house slam shut.

The next morning, she knocked on Kristin's door. Kristin looked happy to see her until she explained why she'd come over. "I need to ask you about the guy next door." Kristin's face fell. "You'd better come in," she said. "This is going to take a while."

Over coffee, Sarah told Kristin what had happened the night before, and heard more than she wanted to. About the neighborhood pets that disappeared after they crossed Barry Finnegan's path. About the doe roaming the neighborhood with one eye, thanks to Barry's air rifle, until she got hit by a car she never saw coming. "As they say on TV, but wait, there's more," Kristin said grimly.

"A year or so ago, Dave and I noticed Barry wasn't alone anymore. There was a nice-looking woman coming and going pretty regularly from Barry's house. We thought, great, he met somebody, maybe he'll mellow out a little." She grimaced. "I always thought there was something to that idea that involuntary celibacy turns men angry. Barry is about the angriest guy I know. I hoped his finally having a woman around would be a good thing. Well, it wasn't. Not for her."

"What happened?" Sarah asked. "The honest answer is, I don't know," Kristin said, her face troubled. "One Saturday night, we heard yelling coming from Barry's. Hers, then his. We walked outside to find out what was going on. We heard the side door slam, and heard her car start up. Then we heard it shut off. We didn't see her leave; we didn't hear anything more. We never saw her again."

"Has anyone gone to the police about any of this?" Sarah asked. Kristin smiled bitterly. "Dave and I were looking for that small town atmosphere, you know? Well, we got it, all right. We went to them after the big Saturday night fight, then again, a week later when our cat turned up dead on our porch. Turns out Barry went to high school with half the cops in the local P.D. They either wouldn't believe he did anything, or they didn't care."

The war between Sarah and Barry began that fall and continued into the following summer. A slow and steady escalation of hostilities. Some tactics would have been routine under any suburban neighborhood Geneva Convention; others were more unorthodox.

Their front yard election signs were, unsurprisingly, diametrically opposed. Courtesy of Barry's complaint to a buddy in the town service department, Sarah got a citation and a fine for putting out her yard waste a day too early for trash day. In turn, Sarah filed a complaint with the town's building department over Barry's peeling house paint and rickety front porch. A week later, she woke to find the word BITCH in bright red paint across her blacktopped driveway.

Kristin warned her to be careful but could not help laughing at some of Sarah's retaliatory strikes. Barry fired his air rifle into Sarah's yard from his second story window, trying to maim the deer roaming her front garden. Sarah got an air gun of her own, aimed carefully through a knothole in the fence, and flattened one of the tires on Barry's pickup.

The wildly expensive peonies she had mail ordered and carefully planted on her side of Barry's fence were dug up and thrown across her front lawn. The next box for Barry mistakenly delivered to her door was carefully placed on his front porch, lightly anointed with just enough dog shit to be overlooked against the brown cardboard. Until you picked it up and brought it closer to your nose.

The conflict grew uglier as winter passed. Leaving the house for work one morning, Sarah found a used condom knotted to her side storm door handle. In turn, Sarah bought a suitably shaped and sized bratwurst at the deli counter, charred it on her stove until the skin blackened and split to show the pink interior, waited until she saw Barry leave in his truck, then put it neatly on his front door sill. With a condom she'd bought at the local drugstore pulled over it.

She also installed an outdoor light of blinding brightness above her side door, one arm of which aimed its bulb upward, squarely at the little upstairs porch outside what she assumed was Barry's bedroom. In all this time, they exchanged not a word. Barry, leaving his driveway in his pickup truck and driving past, would flip her the bird from his driver's side window if she was outside; she would respond in kind, with a double middle finger salute.

As the months passed, she was increasingly aware of how ridiculous the whole exchange had become. She was bothered by the idea that perhaps Barry was actually enjoying all this. In which case, she told Kristin, the best offense might be to declare a unilateral cease-fire. Bullies thrived on attention; the worst thing any bully could experience was indifference. Usually, faced with a lack of response, they would stop trying to get a reaction.

She was right about Barry's need for attention; she was wrong that he would stop.

She was working in her garden again, bent over the spring cleaning of dead leaves and early weeds from her flower beds on the first really warm, sunny Saturday, when she sensed eyes on her. She straightened and looked up at Barry's house. He was sitting on his little upstairs porch, beer in hand, just staring at her. She turned her back on him and went back to cleaning up the beds. Kiss my ass, she thought.

Barry's sitting and staring became a regular thing. Sarah found herself checking his upstairs porch from her own upstairs window before she went outside. Sometimes he was out there, sitting and apparently waiting for her to come out; other times, if he was not there, she'd go outside and begin working, then feel the creeping sensation of being watched. She'd look up, over the fence at the porch, and there he'd be. Staring.

Then he began cleaning his gun ostentatiously while he watched her. No air rifle this; to Sarah's eye, untrained in the identification of firearms, it looked like an AR-15, which she had seen in news coverage of America's seemingly endless series of mass shootings. That spring, Sarah, who had never taken shit from anyone in her life, grew apprehensive, then afraid.

She finally went to the local police department, despite Kristin's assessment that they'd be little help. According to the nameplate on the desk, her meeting was with Deputy Chief Mike Simms. After listening to her lay out the history of her interactions with Barry Finnegan, he gave her the response she already half-expected.

"Look, ma'am, there really isn't much we can do. What you're telling me falls under neighbor-to-neighbor conflict, none of which is actionable unless one of you catches the other breaking the law. He's on his own property, cleaning his own legally purchased firearm as permitted under the laws of this country, state, and locality. Has he ever threatened you directly?"

"Not in so many words, no."

The Deputy Chief stood up and Sarah took that as the signal that their meeting was over. But he waved her back into her chair and crossed the office to the hallway, looked both ways, then shut the door and turned to face her. "I'm going to say this one time, and if you repeat it, I will deny I ever said it. But take this seriously: I am telling you to *beware* Barry Finnegan. I can't give you anything proven to base that on; he's never been convicted of anything, not even arrested. I went to school with him, but that does *not* mean I am his friend. He has always, I repeat *always*, been one mean-hearted sonofabitch. Do not antagonize him further. I will keep my eye on him, but absent a specific threat that is all I can do." Sarah rose from her chair, thanked him, and left.

It was a warm early evening in June when Barry had his accident.

It had rained for two days before that day, and her weeds were running riot. She had been at work all day. Kristin and Dave had left for two weeks to visit family in Maine; Sarah promised to water their plants and take in their mail while they were gone. Before she went over to their house, she wanted to weed her front flower beds while there were a few hours of daylight left. She changed from her office clothes to a grungy t-shirt and shorts she wore for gardening and glanced out her upstairs front window.

Barry was up on his garage roof, hammer and a section of asphalt shingles in hand. Shit, she thought, he had to pick today to fix his goddamn roof. I'll wait a while, she thought; if it's a quick job, I can still get a lot done after he comes down. She went downstairs, got herself a sandwich and a glass of iced tea, reopened the book she'd been reading, and got lost in its pages.

An hour later, her concentration was broken by a yell from next door. She stood and went to the front window. Barry was no longer on his garage roof. She looked at the clock. It was nearly seven; she had about two hours of daylight left. She grabbed her gardening gloves, and her trowel, from the mudroom at her side door, and stepped outside. The sun was still hot.

She stepped into her side yard and heard something unexpected. An agonized moaning coming from behind Barry's gate. "Jeeeeesuuuuuuuus....." She stepped closer to Barry's gate and listened, trying vainly to see into his yard through the narrow gap the gate provided. "Heeeeeeeelp. Meeeeeeeee." The words wheezed and whistled out, punctuated by wet, sucking gasps. She started toward her side door, intending to call 911. Then she heard one more word. "Beeeeeeeeetch."

Fuck you, Barry, she said silently. And wheeled away from Barry's gate and marched to her front garden. Where she worked for the next two hours, as daylight faded, and dusk began to fall. When it was full dark, she finally straightened up and walked to her side yard. She listened at Barry's gate again. Now she heard nothing. She stepped back into her own yard.

In the blue twilight, she saw a silver rabbit. As pale as a drift of smoke and as insubstantial. It hopped toward her and stopped a few yards away, washing its face with its front paws.

She would have thought the rabbit was cute if she weren't able to see right through it.

Something bright at the edge of her vision made her turn her head. A shimmering doe stepped delicately forward out of the bushes at the outer edge of her property. A raccoon she would have sworn was made of moonlight lumbered forward. An opossum and its babies, all in a row. A cat, first one, then cat after cat, all glimmering and rippling in and out of the shadows as she stood there. A groundhog. A plethora of chipmunks and squirrels. A skunk. A fox and its kits.

She gazed around her in wonder, then shuddered, as she realized that each must have met Barry. She looked at the doe again; yes, it had just one eye. At least a hundred different animals were gathered in a semicircle. All staring at Barry's gate. She was reminded, absurdly, of a summer concert, the audience all fixated on the stage, waiting for the star to come out. Sitting vigil.

She heard the latch to Barry's gate click, and saw it begin to open. When she saw the moonlit wisp of woman step through the gate, freed at last, she knew she had been right not to call for help. She would call the police in a day or two, when the smell would confirm what she already knew as the woman and animals drifted and became mist disappearing into the shadows. Barry was gone.

As it turned out, she didn't have to call the police. Two days later, as she was pulling out of her driveway, she saw a police cruiser parked in Barry's driveway. Deputy Chief Simms was getting out of the car. She waved, smiled at him pleasantly, and drove off.

When she returned home, she saw full municipal reaction to an unexpected death in progress. The county coroner's SUV was there, along with an ambulance. Deputy Chief Simms was standing outside talking to a woman wearing a different police uniform than his own; Sarah would learn later that she was from the county Sherriff's office. I guess they found Barry, she thought, and pulled into her driveway.

She was chopping vegetables for her dinner an hour later when the side doorbell rang. She rinsed and dried her hands and went to the door. Deputy Chief Simms stood on her side steps.

"Can I help you?" Sarah asked.

"I'm not sure," he said, "but I would like to talk to you."

"Come in," she said, and led him to the living room. "Please, sit down. Can I get you some water or a Coke or something?"

"No, thank you," he said, and sat down on the edge of her sofa. He held his police officer's cap in his hands, between his bent knees. Sarah sat in silence, waiting for him to speak first.

"Given your history with Barry Finnegan as your neighbor, I'm sure you were wondering about all the commotion next door. We got a call from his workplace when he didn't show up yesterday or today, so I went to do a welfare check this morning." Sarah waited for what she knew was coming next.

"Barry Finnegan is dead. I found him this morning next to his garage."

"What happened to him? He looked fine a couple of days ago."

"I'm hoping you might be able to help fill in some of the details," Deputy Chief Simms said. "Did you see or hear anything unusual next door the last couple of days?"

If you only knew, she thought. "Not really. I did notice he was up on his garage roof working for a while. He had a hammer and some shingles. I did hear a yell a while later, but when I looked outside, I didn't see him on the roof anymore and thought he'd finished what he was doing. Then I went out and worked in the yard for a couple of hours and came inside."

"That's it? You didn't hear or see anything further?"

She gazed at him levelly. "No."

"Well, the yell you heard was Barry falling off the roof. Apparently, he fell right onto the claw of his roofing hammer, which punched right through his stomach and out his back. Based on the signs around the body, we think he may have been alive for an hour or two after that. He probably suffered considerably. That's why I asked if you heard anything more."

111

Revolted, she stared at him, hand over her mouth, nauseated by the image conjured up by his words. "That's terrible," she said, and found she meant it.

"Maybe not," he said, and grimaced.

She looked at him, surprised.

"You and I had a conversation about Barry Finnegan some time ago, and I think you understood that I was concerned about your having any further interaction with him. Your neighbors on the other side met with some of our officers a while before that, to raise concerns about a woman they'd seen coming and going from Barry's place; they were concerned that after what sounded like an altercation one evening, they didn't see her any longer."

"Yes, Kristin told me about that," Sarah said.

"Well, after they took Barry away this morning, I had a look around his house. My last stop was his basement. You know his house is an older one. In the basement there are storage rooms, each with their own door. Back in the nineteen twenties when that house was built, you'd have a pantry in one room in the basement, coal for the furnace in another, and so on." He took a deep breath and paused.

"I found one door boarded up on the outside," he said. "Nailed shut with boards from top to bottom. What I'm going to tell you now is in confidence, and I'm probably breaking every rule in police procedure there is, concerning an ongoing investigation. But you're going to hear it on the six o'clock news soon enough. In fact, you can probably expect the newsies to be knocking on your door for an interview."

"I found a pry bar on his workbench in the basement and started pulling those boards. The door to that room opened outward, so I had to pull off every single one before I could get the door open." He swallowed hard; Sarah saw his Adam's apple move up and down as if he was, indeed, trying to swallow an apple whole.

"There were human remains right behind that door. The coroner will have to confirm it, but based on the clothing that was left, the body was female. My best guess is that she's been dead more than a year, maybe two."

His hands between his knees began a frantic dance, moving around the brim of his officer's cap, spinning it in circle after circle. Sarah saw his eyes filling with tears. He blinked furiously and continued.

"The inside of the door had scratches on it, probably from her fingernails. The coroner thinks she was thrown in there alive and that Barry boarded up the door and let her starve to death. There were no windows, so it's unlikely anyone would have heard cries for help." Sarah found tears running down her own face. She didn't even try to stop them.

"Jesus Christ," she whispered. "Why are you telling me this?"

Deputy Chief Simms rubbed furiously at his own eyes. "Maybe because I feel partly responsible. If we had acted on your neighbors' concerns sooner, we might have been able to save her. I'm going to have to live with that the rest of my life. And I'm sorry I didn't do more than warn you away from him after our conversation."

"But there's one more thing. Given what we found in the basement, we had dogs all over Barry's yard today, just in case anything else turned up. We found a lot of bones, all animals he'd killed over the years. One dog alerted to something by Barry's back gate, so I opened the gate and looked around. There were fresh footprints in the dirt there, from someone standing right next to the gate. The prints look a lot like the sneakers you're wearing right now. And the 911 log didn't show any calls from your address."

Sarah was silent, holding her breath.

"You asked why I told you all this," he continued. "Most of all, I wanted to tell you how glad I am that you let him die."

Doorways
J.S. Rogers

Some people said exorcists were just glorified pest control, but Billie preferred to think of herself as akin to a pet care specialist, like one of those experts hired by people who adopted a puppy that wouldn't stop chewing shoes or a cat that kept peeing in the corner.

After all, no one really trapped ghosts. You couldn't exterminate a spirit. Some exorcists claimed they could, but they were just papering over the problem, easing the symptoms for a while, and kicking the issue down the road for someone else to deal with after everything got worse.

Often, that person was Billie.

She tucked those considerations away as she parked her truly ancient Subaru in front of the old cabin where her job for the day awaited. The owner - some young guy named Dylan who had inherited the property from a great uncle - had called her for help after the last exorcist he'd hired promised results and failed to deliver.

Dylan waited by his vehicle - a dualie with all the upgrades and shiny chrome wheels - and looked nervous, holding a steaming thermos. He was a tall guy, blond hair, with a certain corn-fed scrubbed-clean Midwesterness about him. He did a double take when Billie stepped out, hefting her bag over one shoulder.

Billie'd been told by an ex that *she* looked like she belonged in the corner of a free-trade organic bakery, earnestly singing folk music. She supposed the flowing skirts she favored, when considered with her long, red hair and freckles, gave a certain impression. Her look had cost her work, back in the early days of operating Doorways, but she'd built up a reputation over the years that encouraged clients to overlook her lack of work boots and coveralls.

"Hi, I'm Billie. I hear you may have a problem with a poltergeist?" she said, heading towards Dylan, hand outstretched, bracelets jangling on her wrist. He took her hand with doubt written all over his expression and the door to the cabin slammed open violently, banging up against the wall and belching forth a gust of frigid air.

"Yeah," Dylan said, dry, "you could say that."

***

Dylan inherited the property nearly a year ago, according to the information he shared as they sat in his truck, staring at the cabin. He'd noticed the spectral activity right away, when he stepped inside the first time and a spirit hurled an ancient coffee pot at his head. He sheepishly showed her the scar left behind over his left eyebrow.

"I really want to get the place renovated, but each time I come out here, she does the same thing..." He said, scrubbing at the back of his neck. "So far, no one's been able to help."

"Well, I specialize in tough cases," Billie said, eyeing up the cabin. The spirit continued to toss things around inside, flashes of movement streaking across the windows and past the open door. Highly agitated.

"Yeah, so I heard." He hesitated a moment and then added, "I kind of expected a man."

"Don't worry," she said, restraining an eyeroll that wouldn't be good for business, "the ghosts don't care."

"Right, of course. What do we do, then?"

"*We* don't do anything. I'm going to see if I can learn more about the spirit. I couldn't find any records of murders or other violent crimes on the property." Researching such things was the requisite first step for these jobs. A lack of information made things harder, but not impossible. Plenty of hauntings pre-dated written history, after all, and she'd helped with a few of those. She popped the truck door open and climbed out. "Just wait here."

***

Billie kept her supplies in a repurposed tool box past the back hatch of the car. She popped it open, glancing over sachets, dried herbs, and her five-gallon bucket of salt as she decided what she needed to stuff into the hand-crocheted bag she wore over one shoulder.

"Does *that* ever work?" Dylan asked; she jumped in surprise, looking over as he leaned up against the side of the car. He gestured towards one of the open drawers of her tool box: the one where she stored her pistol when not carrying.

"Not on ghosts." She added some lavender and sage into her bag, along with her packet of white chalk and a bag of ash. The salt she left; she preferred to only use that as a last resort, blocking a spirit out tended to defeat the purpose of trying to determine that they needed to exist peacefully with the living. "But I don't just run into ghosts out here," she added, and took the gun - a little Hellcat that her father had picked out for her after he passed - checked it over, and tucked it into her bag before pulling the rear hatch closed.

"And you know how to use it?" he asked, head cocking to the side.

"Well enough." She tossed some of her hair over a shoulder, arching an eyebrow.

He grinned at her, flirtatiously; he had a charming dimple in one cheek. "Maybe you can give me some pointers sometime, then, I've never gone shooting."

"Maybe," she agreed; relaxing a little. He'd been a little strange since she arrived, understanding that his behavior was attraction-based eased her mind. Plenty of her clientele tried to hit on her, despite her lack of interest. "But for now, you need to go wait in your vehicle. I do assessments with just me and the spirit."

"Yes, ma'am," he said, with another charming grin. He patted the side of her car and ambled off towards his truck. She sighed, hefted up her bag, and set to work.

***

Hauntings happened for all kinds of reasons. Any snags in the fabric between life and death could catch the metaphysical energy released at death and - next thing you knew - you had a ghost hanging around the place.

In most cases, ghosts wanted out of their current situation just as badly as the members of the living around them wanted them gone. Unfortunately, the elemental forces that governed the passage of spirits cared roughly not at all about what anyone thought about the process.

Mostly, ghosts and people just had to learn to live together. That was where Billie came in.

Billie circled the cabin to start, trailing dried lavender behind her, a careful hundred paces out from the building and slowly spiraling inward. She had to make some detours around trees and bushes, looking for the spirit as she worked. She caught a glimpse of the woman only a few times; the ghost stood, frowning and arms crossed, faintly iridescent and not quite opaque. The ghost looked a few inches shorter than Billie, solidly built. The clothing and hair style she'd carried over into death - cargo shorts with a clip hanging off one belt loop, work boots with white socks showing over the top, a plain undershirt with a buttoned-up flannel over top, hair short on the sides with the top combed back - implied she'd probably died sometime in the nineties, or maybe she'd just been behind the times stylistically.

The ghost hadn't thrown anything at Billie's head by the time she reached the cabin. She took a moment to toe off her shoes and sprinkle rose water over her feet before she pushed open the rear door, assessing the dark space beyond and finding disarray. Near everything had been pulled off the walls and smashed against the windows and doors. Most of the destruction looked recent. Dust had yet to settle on the rubble, anyway, while she could see some footprints tracked through the layer of grime on the floor.

Billie sighed and crouched in the middle of the room in a relatively clean spot, fishing out a beeswax candle - she made them herself - and melting the bottom with her lighter, just enough to press it down against the wood floor and make it stick in place.

She lit it, the smell of sage filling the space thanks to the mixture she applied to the wick, and rested on her heels. "Alright," she said, adjusting the fall of her skirt. "Can we talk, then? I know you're around and I want to listen."

The spirit appeared after only a moment, walking right through the wall. She looked at Billie, frowned, and immediately turned to point at the front door, stabbing her finger towards the exit. "Yeah, I get that you don't want people hanging around and I don't blame you." Billie glanced to the side, at the pictures that remained on the mantel, carefully undisturbed amongst the wreckage. "This was your place, huh?"

The ghost tilted her clenched jaw up and pointed towards the door again, jabbing her finger like punctuation.

"It seems like you probably enjoyed your privacy even before. And I get the feeling that you've been here alone a long time. But it's not so bad to let people in, you know. And most people really aren't that bad, once you get to know them."

The ghost crossed her arms and frowned silently, feet planted. "Alright, well, think about it, I guess. I'm just going to check out the rest of the place real quick, make sure there's no one - and nothing - else hanging around. Be out of your hair before you know it."

***

Billie walked out through the front door after she finished looking around the cabin. Leaving took a mighty effort; the ghost held the door shut for a long moment before finally relenting, despite her earlier insistence that Billie leave. The assessment hadn't taken very long due to the size of the building. She found Dylan waiting down off the porch, towards their cars, and walked across the grass to him.

"Well," she said, "you've definitely got *one* spirit. I didn't see any sign of additional paranormal inhabitation. Seems clean of small spirits." She took in his expression and clarified, "Small spirits are the traces left behind by some animals when they die. They can really clutter up some wild areas. And I didn't find any traces of a demonic presence."

"So just the woman." Dylan frowned towards the cabin. "Well, what do I have to do to get rid of her?" The ghost threw something else inside, giving no sign that she planned to ease off.

Billie hid a wince; so often, this represented the

hardest part of her job. "Like I told you before," she said, "just 'getting rid of' a spirit is almost impossible. But I do have recommendations for how you can handle this conflict successfully. I'd recommend that you start with limited interactions to allow the ghost to become used to your presence. Make sure you talk to her, consider leaving some sage sachets; moving in some plants can help. Avoid essential oils in scent diffusers, they tend to just make things worse. She seems protective of the place, I think she must have lived here, so if you let her know you plan to fix it back up, that might help ease some of the tensions."

"And then she'll leave?"

"And then," Billie corrected, "if you both are willing to put in the work, you'll be able to successfully cohabitate. Sometimes ghosts *do* move on, but it's no more up to them than it is up to the living. It's just a matter of patience and, ideally, collaboration. I provide the supplies you should need as part of my contract and offer four mediation appointments as - mostly - the dead don't communicate easily with the living."

"Damn. I really hoped you'd have better news."

"I know it can feel frustrating, but I promise that I can help and–"

"No, you really can't," Dylan interrupted, tone changing as, behind Billie, the door shook and rattled in the frame. "But that's alright. You and I can have a fun time, anyway." He took a step towards her. Billie retreated up to the first porch step. Beside her, one of the yet-unbroken windows shattered. "Yeah," Dylan said, "she *really* doesn't like it when I try to play up here. It's a big problem. I was gonna let you go, if you helped me out."

Ice ran all through Billie's veins. The hair on the back of her neck stood up, mind racing along as she processed what he was saying. Her gut told her that she had no time to question what he meant; she worked with the dead, she had a pretty good idea about his intentions.

Dylan stood directly in the path to her car. He was a big man, built athletically. "Stay away from me," she said, the look in his eyes making her heart beat fast and irregular in her chest. She took a step back, limbs gone clumsy, tripped over the next step, and everything happened all at once.

Dylan lunged towards her, moving terribly fast. She fumbled with the bag at her side, the fabric fighting her attempts to wedge a hand in, while trying to scramble onto the porch. He grabbed her ankle with one big hand, reaching for the strap of her bag with the other, pulling so hard she heard seams burst. She kicked out at him with her free leg, caught his cheekbone with her heel by pure dumb luck, and, when he released her ankle and reeled back, she turned, scrambled up the steps on her hands and knees, and burst through the front door of the house, only realizing as it slammed shut that he'd held onto her bag.

The ghost appeared, her glow lighting up the walls, and pointed urgently at the back door. Later, if she survived, Billie promised herself that she'd process the fact that she'd completely misread this situation, missing the root cause of the ghost's agitation by several miles.

She ran forward, bare feet slapping on wood, as Dylan threw himself at the front door. She heard it rattle and then crack - old wood giving way - before she reached the back door, which stood open and welcoming.

"Come here, you little—" Dylan snarled; she heard objects from around the room smashing into him. The impacts failed to stop him from tackling her, striking the middle of her back; they went down together in a crash against the floor.

She kicked and thrashed, his weight terrible against her back, everything happening too fast to clearly track. She hit something soft with an elbow, and he reeled back briefly, grunting. She managed to twist around, in time for him to grab her, holding her with one hand.

Billie's throat went tight, heart pounding wildly, as she stared down the barrel of her own her gun, dwarfed in his large hand. "Can't even do your job properly," he panted, blood streaming from a fresh cut on his brow. "This is why I have to—"

The ghost shimmered into being behind him, moving

in furious jerks, trying to grip him, spectral hands passing through flesh as broken pieces of glass and wood swirled up off the floor, a tornado contained inside the cabin, whipping viciously through the air. One of the pieces of glass caught Dylan in the back of the hand, sliding into flesh and splattering blood down on Billie.

More importantly, it made him scream as his fingers spasmed open around the gun.

Billie flailed at the falling weapon, caught it in a break of luck, and held her breath as she struggled to situate it properly in her hands, trying to get her finger on the trigger as Dylan reached for it, face contorted with hatred and—

"Oh, shit," Billie panted, after pulling the trigger, stunned. The gun sounded much louder in the little cabin than it had on the shooting range with ear protection. It had kicked, too; she hadn't been in anything like a proper shooter's stance, it had pulled on her arms.

But she'd been shooting at point blank range and none of that had mattered.

Dylan's body swayed and then – blessedly – fell sideways and off her, landing with a bang on the wooden floor. She lay there for a long moment, breathing shallow and shaking all over, watching the swirling wood and glass settle down and trying to keep her heart from pounding out of her chest.

She jolted when the ghost crouched beside her and leaned over into her field of vision, frowning worriedly, and then she made herself sit up, brushed off her skirt, and said, "No, I'm fine. I'm fine. I guess... I should call the police."

***

Billie sat out on the front steps and waited for the cops. The ghost sat beside her, feet planted and elbows on spectral knees, unmoving regardless of how many times Billie said she was fine.

The police arrived eventually in a flurry of flashing lights and confusing questions. The ghost stayed close even then, standing nearby and glowering with her arms crossed while Billie answered questions, accepted a bottle of water, and considered that maybe she needed a lawyer.

In the end, the police left her leave without arresting her, though they made her promise to stay in-state. She agreed and climbed, numb, into her car, glancing at the rearview window as she drove away, still trembling.

The ghost stood watching on the porch until the cabin disappeared around a curve.

**

Life moved on.

It had a funny way of doing that.

Billie hired a lawyer and the court system eventually decided she'd acted in self-defense; it helped that they found evidence of Dylan's previous victims all over his apartment when the police searched the property. Apparently, he'd been looking for a new hunting ground with the cabin.

She tried not to think about it too much, all the mistakes she'd made, the stupid assumptions that had nearly cost her life. She took more jobs, focused on the work, and pushed the nightmares aside as best she could for six months.

When they failed to fade after even that long, she sighed, went out to her car, climbed inside, and headed back to the cabin. The entire business had a feeling of unfinishedness about it, as though she'd left a loose thread hanging; perhaps she just needed to know if the ghost had moved on, now that she'd stopped a serial killer from moving into her cabin.

Worth a shot, anyway.

She arrived with sunset staining the sky all purple and red, putting the car in park in front of the porch. Someone had picked up most of the glass and debris; possibly the ghost herself, now that she no longer had a reason for fury. A sign by the porch said the place was currently for sale.

"This is silly," Billie said, into the quiet of the car. "I should go." She glanced at the porch again, wrestling with herself and the urge that had brought her back to the cabin. She blew out a breath, shaking her head at herself, and pushing the door open, climbing out, pocketing the keys.

She stood there, beside her car, looking at the porch... and as she watched the front door swung open, slow and easy.

And, after all, the living represented only half of those she tried to help. She exhaled and said, "Alright," and went up through the door, to see what had changed.

Veils
Scott J. Couturier

So dulls each candle's lambent flare:
Dims to Darkness every aperture,
Frightful fall of obscure Powers
Telling off these awful Hours.

So comes Doom to my Heart
As Shades from Shadows steal,
Despair manifest, Sorrows made real:

Veils once-hidden hideously part.

Thorns of Life by Sonali Roy

Druden
Herika R. Raymer
Part 3

Lana lay in the hospital bed. The doctors were able to stabilize her, but no diagnosis could be made to explain the odd loss of blood. The patient had no physical trauma, she was just exhausted.

A therapist visited her once she regained consciousness. The patient refused to talk to her. Moreover, Lana ignored her husband's and friends' pleas to accept therapy. They betrayed her. They refused to understand that they took away the only thing connecting her to her daughter. She closed her eyes and sank into immense melancholy as she recalled last night's agonizing events.

"Your daughter waitsss for you..."

Lana's eyes popped open and scanned the hospital room. Initially she saw nothing, but in her peripheral vision something appeared to perch in the shadows in the room's corner. When she turned directly to it, again she saw nothing.

"Want to sssee her?" the whisper enticed.

Her heart raced. Not only at the sibilant voice but also at what it offered.

"Time isss ssshort," it hissed. "Your daughter wantsss to sssee you."

Her eyes filled. Dead Ringer was gone, so Lana would no longer hear her baby's voice. Now, a new opportunity presented itself. Except it was not to just hear her voice, but to see her little girl.

"Yes. Yes, I want to see her," she answered hoarsely.

"Then go to her."

"Where is she?" she asked desperately.

"Lana?" The nurse entered and looked quizzically at her patient. "Who're you talking to?"

She eyed the nurse distrustfully. "Just talking to myself."

The other woman was sympathetic. "You'll be

discharged today. Your husband's on the way."

Lana nodded silently as the woman checked her over one last time.

"Looks good. I'll get you a wheelchair." She smiled. "Be right back."

As soon as the woman exited, the sibilant voice returned.

"Get to Memphisss," it instructed.

Lana's heart thudded in anticipation. When her husband later arrived with the nurse, she meekly obeyed their instructions but her mind spun with plans on how to make the journey to Tennessee. She just needed an opportunity.

"Babe," her husband said tiredly, "maybe we need to get away. Just for a while."

She looked at him and welcomed a thought. "Y-you're right. Time away."

Relieved, he reached over to pat her hand. "I was thinking, maybe the mountains?"

Lana shook her head. "Memphis."

He frowned. "Hon, I don't think-"

"Please." She did not have to fake the pathetic tone of her voice. "Let's go see the ducks."

He regarded her silently for a long time, and then inhaled deeply. "Alright."

Lana smiled and gripped his hand.

'I'm coming, Leah Anne. Mommy's coming.'

***

Laurent and Leig sat across one another at the outside tables of Yollo Rollo. They said nothing as they ate their lunch. Occasionally, Leig checked his phone and then returned to his meal. Laurent idly observed him. Each time the veteran's eyes skimmed to the small device, his stomach tightened.

'What am I doing?' he berated himself. *'I have the item. Time to call the Collector and bounce, as these kids say.'*

On cue, a familiar voice spoke behind him.

"Herr Laurent?"

Etienne paused mid-chew and closed his eyes. *'Of course,'* he bemoaned internally even as he turned towards the speaker.

The messenger bowed his head slightly in respectful acknowledgment. "The item?"

Laurent regarded the man for a few moments before he leaned over to pick up the case which contained the once cursed toy phone. The Hunters assured him the Drude was no longer attached to it. He gathered that also meant that the item most likely no longer had any otherworldly energies attached to it. At least, he hoped so. Until now, he had not thought to ask the Hunters if this was true. Honestly, he figured it was better not to know before he submitted the item. That way he could truthfully say he had no idea one way or the other if ever questioned later.

He wordlessly handed over the suitcase. The Collector's man accepted it with appropriate gravitas. "My employer will be pleased."

Leig smirked behind them.

The well-dressed man handed Laurent a manila envelope."Your payment will be deposited as agreed. Here is the next assignment."

"Wait. What?"

"My employer wanted to be sure to secure your services."

Laurent's brows furrowed but he automatically took the envelope. The little voice in his head grumbled at him, but he was caught unaware. It was reflex at this point.

"*Lebewuhl.*"

The Locator watched the man leave, but unlike previous encounters this time did not have the sense of closure he usually experienced once done with a job for The Collector. If anything, he felt uneasy. As though something were amiss. Though he could not figure out why.

He started when Leig's phone buzzed. He rolled his eyes at his nervousness and shook his head clear of his misgivings. Benavidez's voice spoke through Leig's speaker phone.

"They're leaving."

"Thought they would," the old man scoffed. "Any idea

a direction?"

"They're heading west on Interstate 40. I'll keep with them when I have a better idea. Could be Nashville, Memphis, or even to Louisiana or Arkansas."

"You're our scout, so keep with them. I'll work with the phone."

Laurent's eyes cut sharply at Leig. "Be careful," the young man said.

The old man scoffed again and switched off the phone.

Laurent stared at Leig.

The old man continued to eat, unfazed by his gaze.

The Locator sat and continued to eye the old Hunter warily. The other's nonchalant manner bothered him, especially after what he just heard. His unease increased in the prolonged silence.

"Well then," Leig groaned as he wiped his hands and disposed of his trash. "Time to get to it."

Laurent did not know how to respond.

The older man met his gaze and smirked. There was a wicked gleam in his eyes. Laurent's stomach clenched as Leig's words clicked in his mind.

"When did you switch the phones?" he asked.

Leig grinned without humor. "Can't tell all our secrets, now can I?"

Laurent swallowed hard. "What do you plan to do with it?"

The old Hunter made a shushing motion and then invited the Locator to follow him. Curious, Etienne obeyed. They arrived at Leig's car, a beautifully kept 1968 Plymouth Roadrunner. Once inside, Leig turned on the radio before he turned toward Laurent.

"We're going to use that cursed thing to find the Drude."

The Locator gaped at him. "Are you insane?"

Leig's grin hardened. "Have to be some degree of crazy to answer the Call to be a Hunter." He shrugged. "Here's a free lesson, boy: when something unnatural to this realm, like a demon another type of entity, burrows its way through our natural world, it opens a path. Even when the unnatural entity is removed or destroyed, the path remains. To cut off any more invaders, the path must be destroyed if possible or sealed until such time the path closes again. Unfortunately, such seals must be in place for an extended amount of time. You've seen how some individuals have museums and such, sealing away such items and ensuring regular blessings to keep the seal intact."

Laurent could feel the blood drain from his face as Leig spoke. This was an aspect of the items he Located that he never considered. No wonder Caz thought he was ill-equipped.

"That's one method." The grizzled man's voice broke into his thoughts. He chuckled darkly. "Me? I prefer to melt the doorway shut where possible."

"So you're going to destroy it?"

"Not yet." Leig faced Laurent. "We're going to use it to track down that God-forsaken Drude, along with however many of them have gathered, and destroy the nest."

Etienne's mouth worked a few times before his voice caught up. "H-however many...?"

The old Hunter regarded him. The Locator could see him mentally weighing his next words. The longer he took, the heavier the atmosphere inside the car became. The young man struggled with the urge to open the car door and exit. He could simply leave. The end of this particular chapter would happen, and he would be blissfully ignorant of the contents.

Yet could he do that? With all he knew now, could he just walk away and not know how it ended? There was a hint of a greater problem. At least with the Collector, he knew the ending each time - the item was sealed. Granted, in a macabre museum but still sealed. This time, he was informed the item was only one of a possible flock, for lack of a better term. That meant more cursed items. More pathways to this realm for malevolent entities to cross.

He swallowed hard again. He needed to know how this encounter ended. The next task The Collector wanted him to complete could wait. His fists clenched with his resolve to see this finished.

Leig noticed his action with approval. He nodded.

"Long story short," he supplied, "we've been given reports of other instances of inexplicable illnesses following supposed seances. That's how we followed Dead Ringer here. Except he's not the only one. Whether people feel lost, alone, or inadequate - there is always someone offering a way to fill the void. A predator. Sometimes they work solo, simply presenting a scam. Other times they have a 'helper', like the Drude. The problem we've found is in the reports of too many 'helpers'. And when we isolate the item, the 'helper' flees."

When he stopped, Laurent blinked. He was thoroughly absorbed in what the older man shared. "You think they're regrouping somewhere."

Leig nodded. "You don't go through the trouble of carving a path to a great hunting ground without building a nest somewhere."

"You plan to destroy the nest?"

"That's the plan."

Laurent shivered as cold sweat hugged his clothes to him. "But... Halloween is close."

The other man took a deep breath. "Not an ideal time, granted. However, it's also a time they would not expect to be hit."

The Locator ran a hand through his damp hair.

"Besides," The grizzled Hunter grinned again. "If we destroy it now, the doorway is definitely closed."

Laurent's confusion must have been obvious.

"The Veil." The older man clarified.

'*Of course!*' the younger man thought. '*The Veil is thin during Samhain. That's why it's an ideal time for seances, ghost hunting, and other paranormal or otherworldly activities. So if it's a time for them to build a way in, then it would also be a time to destroy those paths permanently.*'

For the first time since this fiasco began, Laurent felt a surge of hope.

"You coming?" Leig invited.

Etienne did not hesitate. "Yeah, I'm in."

***

Etienne Laurent awoke to the vehicle slowing in front of a motel. Leig quickly put the car in park, exited, and entered. The passenger took the opportunity to stretch and get his bearings. He scanned the area and spied a dog track nearby. It appeared familiar, except his sleep-fogged mind could not quite place it.

"West Memphis."

The Locator turned to The veteran Hunter, who flashed a key card at him.

"Benavidez will join us after he grabs some grub," Leig went on as he re-entered the car.

Laurent followed him, eager to be in a stationary room. Though he was no stranger to long drives, he always appreciated the stops. After five hours on the road, he welcomed the chance to just sit and be still. Not that Leig was bad company, but Laurent had limited tolerance for 70's and 80's music. Since neither man wanted to discuss their respective professions and were disinclined to be overly personal, that left precious few conversation topics until they knew where the Drude lured its victim. The last message from Benavidez stated a stop at Memphis. It was unknown if the river city was the final destination or a stop-over. So, to close the distance, Leig and Laurent drove from Huntsville to Memphis. After more than an hour of classic rock music filling in the silence, sleep was a welcome break. Now they were on the opposite side of the Mississippi River.

"Why West Memphis?" he asked as they pulled into a parking spot close to their assigned room.

"I like being near moving water." Leig answered.

Laurent's brows furrowed again, but the older Hunter said nothing further.

The duo carried their gear into the large room. It only had two beds, but the couch could fold out into a third thankfully. Laurent's bag landed on the couch as a knock sounded. The young man turned to find Leig already seated by the window with his pipe lit. The old man made no move to answer the door. The Locator stood unsure until the second set of knocks sounded. Again, Leig did not move. With a heavy sigh, Laurent opened the door to admit Benavidez. The welcome appetizing aroma of dinner prompted his stomach to complain loudly. The young

Hunter grinned at him.

"Hope you're not too picky," he said as he laid the take out bags on the nearby table. "I wasn't sure what everyone wanted, so I stuck with burgers."

"Meat's always better," Leig grunted and reached for the nearest meal. After a large bite and swallow of the drink, his sharp eyes cut to Benavidez. "Report."

"The woman and her male companion checked in to the Double Tree of Hilton but then made their way to the Peabody."

"The ducks," Laurent muttered.

Both Hunters spared him a look before Benavidez continued. "They are a popular attraction in Memphis, though I'm not sure that's what drew them here."

"They been anywhere else?" Leig inquired.

Benavidez shook his head and took a bite.

"Then it's fair to guess that's a partial reason for their being here. Probably connected to the girl that woman mentioned in the Children's Graveyard."

"Her daughter," Laurent softly reminded them.

Again the Hunters spared him a look. Leig sat back, a half-eaten burger in his hand, and chewed thoughtfully. "Boy's sharp," he complimented the Locator's points. "Too bad you don't have the makings for a Hunter."

Laurent coughed the bite he took and greedily took a long draw from his drink.

Leig smirked.

Benavidez eyed him with interest, shrugged, and picked up the train of thought. "So the Drude lured the woman here with a memory of her daughter. Something Druden excel at. It's how they manage to siphon life out of a target without a fight."

Laurent frowned at the memory of his own encounter with the Drude. It wrapped him in a painful memory, and the enticement to talk to a lost loved one distracted him from what the thing was actually doing to him. From this personal experience, he could easily believe the woman would go wherever the Drude wanted in order to fulfill her psychological need.

"So do we agree this is the final destination?"

Benavidez asked as he crumpled up the wrapper.

"Good bet, based on human nature," Leig agreed while he finished one burger and reached for a second.

Laurent quietly ate and watched the two. He wondered where the toy phone would come into play, to coin a phrase. After all, he needed to know if submitting the wrong item to his client was worth it.

"Don't worry," Leig mumbled. "I'll handle your crazy employer."

The Locator looked at the old man, wondering if he could read minds.

"Not a mind reader, boy," the veteran grumbled as he took another drink. "You've got that pinched worried look, like you know you're in trouble and are trying to find a way out."

Etienne was embarrassed that he blushed at being read so easily. Benavidez chuckled briefly while he also reached for a second burger.

"Yours isn't the first odd collector of questionable paraphernalia," Leig went on blithely, "and, undoubtedly, won't be the last. We've got ways to make them reconsider a particular target."

'*Would've been handy to know back then.*' Laurent thought bitterly. Perhaps if a Hunter had been around during his time in Aztalan, he would not feel indebted to The Collector, a fact that still did not sit well with him. He still waited for the time when she would call in that favor.

"Anyway," Benavidez interrupted as he, too, sat back, "now that we've agreed they've stopped for a time in Memphis, we need to plan out the next steps."

"That's where the item comes in," Leig provided.

This peaked Laurent's attention. He wanted to know how they planned to use the cursed toy phone to find the Drude. The idea was fascinating but also puzzling.

"When's Alexi get here?" Leig asked as he lit his pipe again.

Benavidez peered at his watch before he stood to dispose of their trash. "Anytime. I reached out to him just after I called you."

On cue, there was another knock.

"Speak of the devil." Benavidez grinned and approached the door.

It opened to reveal a young man, same age as Benavidez but with dark sandy blonde hair instead of raven black. His clear blue eyes seemed to shine as he scanned the room's interior quickly and effectively before his gaze focused on Laurent. There was something in that look that made the Locator very nervous.

"He's with us," Leig announced.

The new arrival's eyes shifted to the old Hunter and then he entered. Leig made a gesture which Benavidez managed to decipher and made his way to the older man's satchels. He found the suitcase with the toy phone in it and wordlessly handed it to the newcomer.

Alexi accepted it, placed it on the now cleared table, and carefully opened the case. His features did not change when the seemingly innocent toy phone appeared. He simply stood and stared at it. While he did so, Leig and Benavidez made a circuit around the room. Leig continued to smoke his pipe, while Benavidez rubbed the symbol on his necklace between his fore-knuckle and his thumb. The third man reached a decision just as the pair completed their circuits. He pulled his bag off his shoulder and removed some tools. Laurent blinked at how quickly the men worked, like a finely oiled machine.

He watched as the one he surmised was Alexi began to carefully disassemble the toy phone.

***

The visit to the Peabody proved to be more painful than anticipated.

Lana sat in the opulent grandeur of the Peabody's Grand Lobby, its splendor lost to her. Instead, she focused on the famous water fountain centerpiece where the fabled ducks swam. The bereaved mother could hear her dearly departed daughter's voice giggling. The sound pierced her and kept the wound fresh. The memory of Leah Anne's voice was a pale comparison to the crisp recollections from Dead Ringer's phone. Now, that was gone. There was only the promise that, perhaps, there was another way to connect with her daughter.

"Sssoon," the voice whispered in her ear.

She swallowed dryly. It had repeated that reassurance once they arrived in the Peabody. It startled her at first, mainly because of the silence which accompanied the trip from Huntsville to Memphis. By the time she and her husband pulled into the Double Tree, Lana wondered if she'd hallucinated the voice. Thankfully, she obeyed the impulse to visit the Peabody once they were checked in. The voice hissed to her after she crossed the hotel's threshold. Since the voice had not spoken outside the Peabody, she dared not leave it. At least not yet. As a reward, periodically the whisper would assure her the reunion would happen soon. Yet how soon? Lana's eagerness to see her daughter again made her edgy.

"Baby."

She did not move when her husband spoke to her.

He sighed heavily. "You haven't eaten all day. It's eight o' clock. C'mon. Let's grab a bite."

Lana refused to acknowledge him. Her eyes were fixed on the water fountain.

He gingerly but firmly took her elbow. "Sweetie, we need to go."

The idea of leaving was repugnant, his touch unwelcome, the idea of eating nauseating. She wanted, no, *needed* to stay. The voice said she would see Leah Anne soon.

"Give him a tasssk," the voice instructed.

Lana blinked, unsure what to do. Then she mentally grabbed onto the last thing he said. He wanted to eat. They were in a luxury hotel. Surely there was a restaurant. With effort, the bewitched woman turned to her husband and smiled. "Let's just grab something from the restaurant, yeah?"

He paused, his hand still on her elbow.

"I just want to stay a bit longer." She allowed a note of pleading to seep into her tone. "I don't have much of an appetite. How about a turkey club or maybe a large salad with chicken. Something light?"

Her husband hesitated a moment longer, but then returned her smile with a wane one of his own. His looked resigned, and her heart went out to him.

For a moment, she wanted to share the possible gift with him, the idea that they both could see Leah Anne together was enticing. Then she recalled how he kept trying to get her to accept their daughter's death and move on, as if it were that easy. How he scoffed at the idea that she could hear her child's voice. Those memories closed the door and boosted her resolve to send him away from her.

"Alright, hon." He nodded, leaned over to kiss her forehead, and walked towards the restaurant.

"Now," the voice hissed, "leave this plasss and follow my directionsss."

Immediately, Lana stood and exited the Peabody while summoning an Uber. Fortunately, one was nearby. It picked her up before her husband had a chance to discover her absence. The whispers gave directions, which she repeated to the driver. Soon, she found herself in midtown Memphis, along Central Avenue, and dropped off at one of the smaller eateries. Only, she did not stop there. Instead, she walked along the darkened and lonely streets until she found the abandoned grounds. The rusted gates seemed to open for her and she made her way along the chipped yet somehow still vibrantly painted structures of the old amusement park.

The whispers guided her to the dilapidated carousel.

"Ssshe'sss there," it promised.

Lana smiled.

***

Alexi hissed.

Leig and Benavidez looked at him sharply. The toy phone lay in a deliberately organized mess inside the silver case Laurent originally carried it in. The third Hunter froze in place above a portion of the small receiver he managed to remove.

'Who could have guessed something made in the time of World War II was still in such pristine shape?' Laurent wondered, despite his awareness of the inanity of such thoughts at this time.

"I take it you got something?" Leig prompted.

Alexi nodded. "This is the piece which collected the most energy from the victims." He gestured to the piece.

"Why do I get the feeling there's a reason you hissed?" Benavidez pressed.

Alexi's eyes moved from the part to his comrades. "It's active."

The energy in the room charged unpleasantly.

"It's getting ready to feed." Leig groused.

"Then now's the time to move, right?" Laurent asked.

The other men were already in motion. Leig and Benavidez gathered their smaller bags while Alexi placed the small toy part on a strange container. It was not until Alexi put on the top that Laurent recognized the compass rose which adorned it.

"How much time do you think we have?" Benavidez asked as he and Leig crossed to the door.

"Imagine it don't matter," Leig growled. "We need to be more focused on how many are there."

Laurent trembled as he stood and watched the three Hunters grab their gear. Alexi carefully carried the peculiar compass which used the toy receiver piece as its magnetic north. He spared the Locator a pointed look, and nodded to the silver case. Instinctively, Etienne carefully closed the case to preserve the cursed item as much as possible and carried it out of the room. He followed the three Hunters into Leig's Plymouth. Leig and Alexi were in front while Laurent and Benavidez rode in the rear.

Leig drove back across the bridge into Memphis. Once there, he followed Alexi's directions as best he could. They avoided the highways, not enough turn offs, and kept to the roads in the city. Laurent was not surprised to find them traveling along Southern Avenue and past the more abandoned areas of the once great city.

Eventually they pulled into what looked to be an abandoned landmark. The Locator and three Hunters exited the vehicle. Alexi led the way, slowly sweeping the peculiar compass to ensure they went in the proper direction. Laurent felt a heaviness in the air. He scanned the area in the hopes of finding something to help identify the area and found a historical marker immortalizing the resting place of Libertyland.

The first hint of the rotten egg smell wafted towards the quartet. The Locator recalled it from the Dead Children's Playground. The chill Laurent felt had nothing to do with the weather.

It deepened as he followed the Hunters further onto the decrepit grounds. Alexi did not rely as heavily on the strange compass, but as the odor grew stronger he made sure they kept on target. Idly, Laurent wondered if flashlights would be useful at this point. However, the trio appeared to prefer the use of moonlight. He dared not say anything but simply followed their lead.

Finally, they stood before the rickety carousel. The overpowering stench caused Laurent to cough. Though he had no 'special' sight, he swore the old amusement park ride fluttered slightly, as if being seen through a heat haze.

Benavidez made the sign of the cross.

Alexi froze and scowled.

Leig growled something under his breath.

Knowing the Hunters for the brief period he had, Laurent guessed it was most likely Scripture. After all, despite whatever happened Laurent never heard any of the Hunters curse. Not even in passing or in jest. The Locator focused his attention on the decaying structure. After some heartbeats, something flickered in his vision.

"There you are..." a familiar hiss sounded.

The icy grip of fear encompassed Laurent.

"Come to sssee your beloved?" it taunted him.

Cold sweat ran down his skin as a chorus of hiss-like laughter followed the taunt. It was as the Hunters warned him. Except it was one thing to suspect, yet another to know.

The Drude was not alone.

***

Etienne Laurent gaped at the sight before him.

In addition to the putrid stench, the merry-go-round's paint was chipped in some areas and fluttered sickly in others. The faded colors and exposed areas gave the carved horses a garish look. Goosebumps tickled his flesh as Laurent continued to stare at the dilapidated wooden figures. They seemed to snarl at him from within their shadows.

He took a shallow breath when their blank eyes flared to life.

Not all of them, but several of the still equines glared at the four men using the eyes of their newly acquired riders. Though he never claimed to have special sight, just like before Laurent could distinguish their stygian silhouettes against the dark backdrop. It was eerie to see black upon black.

"Etienne," they hissed in unison, only it did not sound like separate voices in chorus. Instead he heard one voice. He shook at the familiar tones.

"Etienne," Nat's voice called to him. "You've come to me?"

He stood transfixed. There was no way she was here. She was dead. Yet, he heard her voice. The shadows moved, and he could swear he could make out a human silhouette in the darkness. His heart skipped unpleasantly at the thought Natalie was here. The longing resurfaced, demanding to be fulfilled. It was now or never. He could finally say what he wanted to!

He started as the three men began to sing low. Their words were soft and unintelligible. It took him a few moments to realize the latter was because they were speaking in another language, one he was not familiar with. As they did so, Alexi and Benavidez took action. Leig stood his ground as the two young Hunters walked in opposite directions and made their way around the cursed carousel. All three still had their light carryovers, but at present were more focused on maintaining their song as they walked.

His eyes, initially glued to the silhouette, darted between the three men. Their song managed to penetrate the hisses of the Druden. When he looked back, the silhouette was still there. What should he do? Was it really Nat? He did not think so. The Hunters said the Druden induced a dream-like fugue in its victims to feed off their life. If he conjured an image of Nat, then they had gotten him into a dream-like state. With that realization, he felt like he was in a waking dream. He felt himself getting tired.

Not for the first time, Laurent wondered why he was there. He was not a Hunter. He had no idea what he was supposed to do.

The Hunters' song became more pronounced, diverting the attention of the Druden.

The Druden snarled and hissed at their adversaries. Initially, they tried to lure the men with promises of contact with any loved ones. When these lures fell on deaf ears, and the men continued their circuit, the creatures began to hurl curses instead.

"Go away!"

Laurent started when the woman's voice shouted from the silhouette within the structure.

She stepped out of the shadows, holding one of the Drude in her arms. It's darkness wrapped around her as if it were embracing her. She clutched at it as she glared at the men. "You're not wanted here! Leave us alone!"

'*Us?*' The Locator wondered. Puzzled at the term, he looked around to see if there was anyone other than the Hunters, himself, and the woman from Huntsville. Seeing no one else, he turned again to her.

She held the Drude close to her and murmured something to it. "It's okay, sweetie. I won't let them hurt you."

Laurent felt his stomach clench. '*Dear God,*" he realized, "*she thinks the demon is her daughter.*' The implications of this were horrid. The woman paid an expensive fee to Dead Ringer to simply talk to her deceased daughter. Now deceived into thinking she held her precious child once more, how dangerous would she get?

Alexi and Benavidez ignored her just as they ignored the hissing Druden. They kept a steady pace to complete the circle. Their action appeared to agitate the bereaved mother more. Laurent glanced at Leig, who - like the younger two - had not stopped singing. The older man met his gaze and cut his eyes to the woman.

'No.' Laurent thought grimly. *'Surely he does not expect me to deal with her.'*

Leig nodded firmly to the woman again, looking pointedly at Laurent.

The Locator cursed silently, not daring to voice his sentiments aloud. Just how was he supposed to handle a grief-stricken mother bewitched by a Drude into thinking the small demon was actually her departed daughter? The idea was daunting to say the least. Especially with the combined effect of the Druden continuing to drain his own energy.

"Mommy?" the thing said in an eerie girl's voice. "I'm ssscared."

The woman's arms tightened. "It's okay, baby. I won't let them hurt you."

Alexi and Benavidez approached the halfway mark as they continued to walk at a steady pace and sing lowly. Leig and the woman's gazes locked in an unspoken battle of wills. Her eyes still glanced warily at the two young men to either side of her, but her focus appeared to be mostly on the grizzled man before her.

"Mommy!" the Drude whimpered in the girl's voice as it tightened its grip around her neck. "Why are they walking behind us? Are they going to hurt us?"

The creature succeeded in distracting the woman from Leig to the two young men. Her unease magnified as the Drude mimicked a little girl whimpering with fright. Her head switched rapidly between the two men, who paid her no mind as they worked to complete their task.

"What are you doing?" Fear lined her voice when she addressed the trio.

They never broke their song.

"Why are you singing?" Panic crept into her voice as it raised.

Laurent pushed through his growing weariness and cautiously moved forward, thankful her focus did not waver from the three Hunters. Adrenaline must help her fight the effects of the Druden. Either that, or they were intentionally not feeding off her. Then again, it could be a combination of both.

"Stop!" she yelled frantically as she hugged the Drude.

"Mommy?" it asked tremulously. The other Druden gathered around her and began to hiss in unison with the one in her arms. "What's he doing?" they asked. "He's scaring me."

Her head swiveled between the three men, one stationary and the other two making their way beyond the half-way point. Laurent still went unnoticed. He was not sure if that was a good thing or not.

"Why's he trying to get behind us?" they asked collectively in a girl's voice which echoed eerily. "What's he going to do to us?"

The implication that the Hunters meant harm was so pronounced that the woman's body stiffened visibly. Laurent felt his own body tense at her reaction. The Druden were pushing her to act. Why? Did it not want the young men to finish their circuit?

"Mommy!" They practically begged the panicking woman. "Stop him!"

"Ok, ok, baby," she soothed in a shaky voice as she set the Drude down. "Mommy's got this."

In a blink, she rushed Benavidez. Laurent reacted instinctively and ran to intercept her. Thankfully, Benavidez was on the side closer to Laurent. The Locator managed to tackle the woman before she could reach him. He had no idea if Benavidez was even aware of the drama behind him since he kept moving.

"Let me go!" the woman screamed as she struggled against his grip.

Though he prided himself on his physical fitness, there was no better test of this than the attempt to restrain an uncooperative subject while not harming them. By nature, a man is stronger than a woman. No matter what popular culture tried to say, this was a simple biological fact. Still, desperation gave individuals crazy strength and agility. This woman was desperate, and her goal to stop Benavidez gave her incredible focus towards that adrenaline-fueled end. He might have been more effective if the Druden were not feeding off him.

Still, he had his own goal: to keep the woman from

Benavidez. Or Alexi. Or even Leig. They had to finish whatever they were doing.

She managed to get on her hands and knees under him. He locked his arms around her waist and planted his foot to their side. He grunted as he pushed with his foot and toppled them over. Growling at her, he manipulated her struggles to where her back was on his chest. He then looped his arms under hers and locked his hands behind her head. It was an old restraint, but usually effective. He also locked his legs around her waist from behind.

Laurent made himself an anchor.

Whenever she tried to roll over so she could get up, he used his weight to keep her in place. She screamed, cursed, elbowed his sides and kidneys, and even tried to turn her head enough to bite into his arm. All the while, he focused his fading strength into keeping her in place.

"Anytime now guys," he stammered while he held onto the human live wire.

The Druden's miasma thickened. An unpleasant blanket settled over him. It was almost suffocating. The heaviness of sleep tempted him, but he refused to submit. He just needed to hold on a bit longer.

"Mommy!" the Druden hollered helplessly as they played on the poor woman's delusion.

"Bastards!" the woman screeched. "Leave my baby alone!"

"That thing isn't your daughter!" Laurent finally managed to yell in her ear.

"Shut up!"

"She's dead!" he went on.

"No!" Her tone changed to a panicked denial. "She's there! You see her! She's there!" She stopped struggling long enough to point to the cursed carousel, where the Druden gathered.

Laurent's heart went out to the woman, but he had to continue. "She's dead."

"No!" she screamed. "Leah Anne! Tell him!"

At that moment Alexi and Benavidez reappeared on opposite sides of the merry-go-around yet this time facing towards Leig rather than away.

"Mommy!" the Druden called to the restrained woman.

"Let me go!" She rolled with Laurent in a panicked surge of strength.

Taken aback, the Locator could only hang onto her and continue her motion so that she was unable to get enough purchase to throw him. They rolled into Alexi's path. He approached with the steady pace he and Benavidez had kept since they started the circle. His eyes flashed at the pair of them in his way. Somehow, Laurent knew he had to get them out of the way. He attempted to roll them out of the path, but even as he was able, the woman counteracted it. He did it twice before he realized his dwindling strength could not keep this up.

Alexi was almost upon them. Laurent knew he only had enough strength left to move her one more time. So he had to time it perfectly.

The woman was already screaming at Alexi and reaching out to him. Her hand curled into claws to latch onto and gouge his legs. The Druden hissed curses at the men while whimpering cries of help to the woman. It amazed Laurent how she was deaf to one and tuned into the other. Then again, the Druden's influence on their victim most likely filtered out anything that would be detrimental to their goal. She probably couldn't even hear the cruelty spoken by the shadow-like creatures. Thankfully, her focus had an advantage for Laurent. With it centered on Alexi, she was unable to resist his push to roll them out of the way.

"No!" she screamed as Alexi walked passed them.

The young men were almost to where Leig stood. Their voices became even louder. The song soothed Laurent as it helped ease the effect of the Drude's drain.

The Druden screeched then. A sound akin to bats fleeing a cave. The miasma thickened horribly. Laurent tightened his grip as much as he could on the woman. It was difficult to get a good grip on his coat sleeves, but somehow his clothes sticking to his sweat-drenched skin helped keep the cloth in place. She continued to struggle, but it seemed weaker this time.

"Mommy!" they called to her as the young men met

with Leig. "Help us! They want to take me away!"

"No!" she cried. "Don't take my baby!"

Laurent once wondered how cruel a Drude could be. He now had his answer. Their inhumanity astounded him.

"Leave her alone!" the desperate mother shrieked.

"She's dead," Laurent reminded her as he held on.

"She's alive!" she retorted hotly. "I won't lose her again! I'll gladly trade my life for hers rather than lose her again!"

Laurent shuddered as the miasma coalesced around them. His skin was clammy with cold, and he wondered if he would ever feel warm again. He stole a look to the three Hunters. Though their song never faltered, their faces shared a grim shock that bothered him. Laurent knew words had meaning, especially when dealing with cursed items.

This woman just offered to trade her life for an illusion.

And monsters do not take such offers lightly. The Druden meant to collect. Especially since they now faced Hunters bent on their demise. They needed the energy.

The miasma's fog folded around the woman like an ethereal blanket. Its chill cut into him, even though the fabric of his coat. He could not release her and scurry away fast enough. Her eyes widened as it enveloped her. Her mouth opened in a silent scream. Laurent could only watch helplessly as her skin went from a angry red from their fight, to a healthy pink, and finally to an ashen pale. The victim barely had time to register what had happened.

Laurent's eyes then went to the Hunters.

They still sang. Their bags were at their feet, their hands held before them with palms up, and their eyes open. He watched as the Druden gathered from all corners of the cursed carousel. They all faced their mortal foe. Their eyes glowing red. Ancient. Hungry. Terrible. Even though they were not focused on Laurent, he still felt the malevolence of their gaze.

The shadows gathered around the Druden. It coiled and spun, gathering intensity. Soon, it was as stygian black as the creatures who manipulated it. The darkness pulsated with evil. Fueled by stolen lives and directed by the will of the demons, the blackened energy awaited a command.

"Look out!" Laurent yelled as the tension in the air snapped.

Simultaneously, the pitch shot out from the cursed carousel towards the Hunters.

Incredibly, Laurent watched as the malignant energy crashed against a luminescent shield before the trio. The wave coalesced on the celestial surface and then began to shimmer and clear. The cleansed energy turned back towards the Druden. The demons screamed as the energies, now purified and Blessed by their Song, flowed back towards them. They tried to escape, but it was futile.

The energies enveloped the cursed carousel. It washed over the wooden horses and lit up all the pillars. When it touched the Druden, their blackened bodies cracked as if they were burned logs, turned gray, and crumbled apart like ashes. Yet even the flakes were not allowed to flutter away. Instead, they were absorbed in the light. As the light faded, the carousel returned to its dilapidated state. Only now, the acrid sulfur stench dissipated.

Eventually, the Hunters lowered their hands.

Only then did Laurent move. He got to his feet and warily approached the trio. He looked over at the carousel, and then at them again. He dared not ask if it was over, just in case the answer was not what he hoped.

Alexi pulled out the strange compass and swept it across the area. It did not act as it had before. It merely pointed in whichever direction he had it.

The three men relaxed visibly.

Laurent let out the breath he did not know he had been holding.

"Let's go," Leig commanded as he retrieved his small bag.

Wordlessly, the young men mimicked him and fell into line behind him.

Laurent looked back and forth between them and the structure. He had questions, and now seemed the only chance to ask.

"So it really is over," he managed weakly.

Benavidez paused and turned to him. His eyes slid from the Locator to the carousel. "Yes, it is."

He looked at the prone figure on the ground. "Her?"

The young man followed his gaze. "We'll contact the husband."

Laurent looked at Benavidez, alarmed. If the husband suspected foul play, there was enough physical evidence from him to make him a prime suspect. He had no desire to get embroiled with law enforcement.

Benavidez smiled tiredly. "We'll handle the details. Don't worry." He indicated for Laurent to join them as he turned to catch up with Leig and Alexi.

Each step became less of an effort the more he moved, a clear indication the Drude's spell was wearing off. Or perhaps an aftereffect of their Song. Recalling how he passed out and then woke up in a hotel room due to one Drude, Laurent was pleased he would not need any such care this time. Still, the items had claimed one life. What if it was hungry for more?

He eyed the man beside him. "The... the carousel?"

By this time they caught up to the other two. Leig answered as Benavidez put his bag in the trunk with the other two. "Carousel's been neutralized."

"The pathways?"

"Cut off."

Laurent spied the bags before the trunk lid closed. "You didn't use those."

"They're for dealing with any human element," Benavidez supplied.

"You took care of that." Leig smirked as he pat Laurent on the shoulder before he entered the Plymouth.

The Locator blinked and then followed suit.

As the quartet left the site, he turned over the events in his head. He believed Leig and Benavidez when they said they would handle the details. Not just about the woman but also about the cursed toy phone and, undoubtedly, the carousel. Though he was curious what they would tell The Collector, he had no plans to be a part of that conversation.

Laurent's focus inward muted his surroundings. He heard Benavidez make a phone call but pointedly paid no attention to the details. He knew it had to do with the woman and her husband because that had to be handled directly. However, the less he knew about how Hunters covered their tracks, the better. The matter was resolved by the time the Plymouth crossed into West Memphis.

Oddly enough, the Locator did fell better when they were on the opposite side of the river. By the time they arrived at the motel, he could barely keep the exhaustion at bay. The bed called to him, and he wanted to answer.

The men exited the vehicle. Leig, Benavidez, and Laurent entered the room but Alexi departed. His part was done. Laurent barely had the energy to thank the Hunters before he collapsed on the bed.

He awoke mid-morning to an empty room. Confused, he looked around but found no sign of his roommates. Their items and the Plymouth were gone. He rubbed the back of his neck, but completed his own preparation to leave, which included calling an Uber.

As he turned in his key card, the receptionist handed him an envelope while wishing him a good day. Curious, he exited the hotel before he opened it. The scrawl was barely legible, but he managed to decipher it.

"Good job, Locator. I stand by what I said, you'd make a fair Hunter. A good one with proper training. You ever get the Call, wait for me. I'll find you. In the meantime, pay more attention to your surroundings. The Truth is in front of you. Take care you're not easily deceived. And, just maybe, stop taking commissions from that crazy woman you call a boss."

Laurent chuckled at the last part. He toyed with the same thoughts, but inevitably ended up working for her. He wondered what it would take for him to finally stop accepting her commissions. He recalled the manila envelop waiting in his overnight bag. The one her lackey brought after the encounter with Dead Ringer.

Maybe it would be the one.

Maybe.

ARTICLE

Ghosts Can Exist!
Sonali Roy

Rationalism never permits the existence of ghosts or spirits. Even, mere thinking of them is considered as silly because those are the manifestations of superstitions, omens, and some medical issues. Many of us question about the existence of ghosts- even some hang in between to be or not to be. Some skeptics have also experimented with the concept. But, what about those really faced such ghostly encounters? Generally, ghosts are aerie- we cannot touch them, and they can be everywhere. Personal accounts report that we can realize their existence though cannot see them. But, it is logical. For instance, we can never see air (nor ever would be able to do so!). But, it's not that air does not exist. We assume mild breeze is blowing over the paddy fields or the mustard flowers that we see them stirred. Not only that, but think of the oxygen we breathe of- yes, we're making a nonstop exhaling & inhaling of air. Then, what does it indicate? It's indicative of the already present air within all of us- the entire animal kingdom- that we cannot see. When you stop exhaling & inhaling, you're taken as dead. So, it is clear that the air present within all of us is the sole energy that makes us alive- without it, we are dead. So, if air is energy, science definitely permits the transformation of energy and that energy never ends up. You've definitely heard of the transformation of energy- say of solar to electric, water to thermal, wind to thermal, and so on. Also, science allows the cycling process- say of oxygen, carbon, and nitrogen cycles. To sum up, nature's objects and elements cycle & recycle and mix up into the same. So, nothing ends up in the strict sense of the term. Some ancient scriptures also advocate the existence of energy and souls. So, if air is soul, that is, energy, it can be transformed. And also that air can travel everywhere. And evidently, ghost can also exist because though after the bodily death, energy can exist and travel everywhere. It happens sometimes that you took the photograph and discovered someone in the frame who is already dead. Yes, it's the spirit, ghost, unidentified object, entity, energy, or soul- whatever you may call it. Some find the scratches on their hands and legs that they can't identify. Maybe, these can be due to ghostly phenomena.

After the death of my dear canine friend Fuchoo, I got the smell of his body (that I brushed him with the talc on that very day of his departure) just on the night of his death. Not only that, after the death of my grandmother, I got the smell of her body for nearly two months or so. And, all of us still witness some weird activities (you may call these uncanny and paranormal) in this house- we are still threatened with some unexpected and sudden occurrences. I hear my mom often narrate a story that when she was a teenager, a girl of sixteen in their locality was possessed by an evil spirit. And a sage cured her of this. People believe that souls with good activities and intention in their bodily forms still do good in their aerie existence. So, after death, living creatures can survive as spirits. Besides, people sometimes report they see the spirits fully clad in clothes. Is it possible? Some think that these out-of-body experiences are possible, whilst, others consider these as purely illusory, or something related to clairvoyance or the mediumistic world. Yes, I never saw any spirits clad in clothes. What I experienced about them is that I felt some cooler air, some creaking sounds without anybody seen, sigh of breathing, or some other unusual things. For instance, my grandmother died on January 1, 2014 in the morning. When I went to the kitchen at night for boiling some rice, I felt someone was near me and breathing over my shoulder. I looked back, but found none. I assumed my stressed mind could lead to such illusions. Later, I went to filter the rice, and the container somehow slipped from my hands. But, most surprisingly, the rice remained the same in the container, and not a single grain dropped on the floor. But, whenever I saw the dead persons in my dreams, they were all clad in clothes as they were while living. Whenever I dream such, something problematic occurs, e.g. sickness of any family member, some problems in the professional front, some accidents, or the like. So, I feel terrified at such dreams, although my father says that dead persons come in dreams to hint at the upcoming problems, or that they appear in our dreams to indicate all your worries would soon come to an end. Maybe, the spirits try to convey their message through dreams, or simply they would like to guide you.

Anyways, let's come back to out-of-body experiences. It happens many times that you are thinking of someone else, and right then, he/she is there in front of you, or calls you on phone. According to psychology, it's known as telepathy. Notably, the person you were thinking of was not present there at the time of your thinking about him/her. Some believe that it's our subconscious mind or the sixth sense that can predict the future through some dreams and symbolisms, some unusual phenomena, or the like. Telepathy occurs in case of living bodies. But, what about those departed this world?

Externalists believe that the human mind "is essentially and inseparably bound up with some kind of extended quasi-physical vehicle, which is not normally perceptible to the senses of human beings" (Braude, S.E. (2003). *Immortal Remains: The Evidence for Life after Death.* Lanham, Maryland, USA: Rowman & Littlefield).

Ghost-hunters investigate paranormal cases by using certain things like electromagnetic field meters, infrared meter, audio enhancer, electrostatic generator, strobe light, tone generator, and dowsing rods etc.

Some consider spirits as electromagnetic energies. So, paranormal investigators use electromagnetic field meters to identify the changes in the electromagnetic energies. Infrared meters are used for measuring changes in heat sources. For enhancing hardly inaudible voices, ghost hunting teams use audio enhancer. Electrostatic generator sprays ions into the air and unties natural electric bonds. This should elevate ghostly activities if electrostatic charges influence the materialization of ghosts (Warren, Joshua P. (2003). *How to Hunt Ghosts*, p. 178.).

It should also be noted that if you are threatened with paranormal fear, you may feel/and experience like the paranormal. In that case, your anxiety and stress may lead to such happenings. Or, your extreme fear of darkness can make you hallucinate or feel surrounded by spirits. In some cases, I noticed that persons too much affected by deaths, accidents, or anything like these suffer mostly from the unusual phenomena. Or maybe, they are too influenced by myths, legends, horror movies, or stories that they create an imaginary world of their own- the characters, settings, and events of the stories greatly impact them. Even, they can hardly come out of this imaginary world. And this is a different case. Moreover, if you are too much taken by negative thoughts, you are more likely to undergo such ghostly and terrible experiences. My parents say that the more you are possessed by negative thoughts and feelings, the more the negative energies can dominate over you. And I can't deny that. If you develop positive attitude to life, the negative spirits can hardly win over you. Actually, the universe runs on two principles- positive and negative- as is of the electrical engineering context. And the paranormal world is no exception of it. But, at the same time, something happens that we can't always explain.

Apart from personal records, there are also some scientific researches that prove the reality regarding this. Dr. Barrie Colvin once said,

> "The sounds produced by 'ghosts' during hauntings are paranormal. Their acoustic waveforms are completely different. I cannot find a conventional explanation for my results at all. Nor can any of the other scientists who have reviewed my work. To be honest, we are completely stumped. We did not expect to find these results".

There is also ample evidence that attest the existence of ghosts, as for instance, the proofs as collected by the ghost hunting team TAPS or The Atlantic Paranormal Society. If an area of a room or a house is possessed by ghostly phenomena, the temperature of that portion is likely to be cooler than any other areas of the room or the house. If they feel any unusual or other-worldly atmosphere, The Atlantic Paranormal Society use digital thermometer to record the temperature of the area. The team uses electromagnetic field meters to trace ghostly existence,

> "because the EMF meter will have a very high reading in the vicinity of a lot of electrical equipment or wiring or in the presence of a ghost. TAPS, as well as other teams, will check for electrical wiring to make sure that there is no interference when they receive a high reading on the EMF meter" (https://www.atu.edu/worldlanguages/texts/atuw-2019/I06r.pdf).

For identifying specters, the society uses thermographic and night vision cameras. Thermographic cameras have infrared radiation, which displays the temperature of an object. With the night vision cameras, the team can see what they would not find in darkness. The team can also determine the ghostly movements with these cameras. With these devices, the team has shown that there is something beyond this world that could appear/and seem to be absurd or other-worldly. The inaudible/and whispering and aerie phenomena is also a science.

Some may doubt their existence, but still though spirits exist!

Further Readings:
https://the-atlantic-paranormal-society.com/the-mystery-of-the-teleporting-man-who-vanished-the.an-re-appeared-500-miles-away/
https://www.atu.edu/worldlanguages/texts/atuw-2019/I06r.pdf
https://psi-encyclopedia.sprc.uk/users/barrie-colvin
https://psi-encyclopedia.spr.ac.uk/articles/why-do-ghosts-wear-clothes

ARTICLE

The Most Haunted Places in Brazil
Livian Bonato

Brazil is a Latin American country known for its natural beauty, forests, beaches, carnival, and parties. But is that really all? Discover some of the most haunted places in the country, from a ghost riding a neighing horse to one of the largest reported alien sightings ever.

Joelma Building

The Joelma Building in São Paulo was the site of a tragic disaster: On February 1, 1974, a fire started on the 12th floor, quickly spreading throughout the building. The fire killed 191 people and left 300 injured, many of them seriously.

Before the construction of the building, at the end of

the 19th century, there was a whipping post (a place for public punishment of criminals) on the site, and later, it is said that a man murdered his mother and sisters before committing suicide.

Today, the building is open as a commercial space, where people still report hearing voices, moans, and feeling a heavy presence in the elevator, where several people died trying to escape. The elevator is said to stop at random floors, with its doors opening and closing repeatedly.

Another reported phenomenon involves the "13 souls," referring to 13 people whose bodies were never identified because their remains were fused together. They had tried to escape via the elevator, but the cables broke, causing them to fall freely through the building.

The bodies are buried in São Pedro Cemetery, where they are revered as miracle workers. Their screams are still heard, which only cease when people pay their respects.

The Cavalier of Jaraguá

In Jaraguá, Goiás, residents claim that the entire block on Rua das Flores is haunted. The most notable phenomenon is the constant sound of a horse trotting at night, accompanied by the jingling of spurs, an inexplicable chill, and unsettling sensations. On the horse, a man dressed in an elaborate riding outfit can sometimes be seen. He is said to be a nobleman who died, remaining trapped between worlds.

Have you heard the legend that if someone dies with many material possessions, they are unable to let go of them and become a ghost? Well, perhaps this explains why there are so many reports of ghosts from the nobility.

Vale do Anhangabaú

In São Paulo, the Vale do Anhangabaú has been the site of numerous suicides over the years. The origin of the name in Tupi-Guarani means "water of the evil spirit," as a stream once flowed through the area where, according to legends, many indigenous people drowned while trying to escape the slavery imposed by Europeans during colonization. There are countless reports of people hearing the sounds of spirits passing through the area, as well as a dense energy that permeates the place.

Consolação Cemetery

Consolação Cemetery, in São Paulo, is the resting place of many notable figures, such as writer Monteiro Lobato, Mário de Andrade, Tarsila do Amaral, Ramos de Azevedo, the Marquesa de Santos, Líbero Badaró, and Dona Yayá.

It is said that during the burial of the noble Matarazzo family, a gravedigger suffered a heart attack and died. According to visitor reports, he continued to work hard after death, being seen with his shovel. Additionally, ghosts are reported to chase visitors, tormenting them with voices, whispers, and lamentations.

The famous figures buried there, as well as a child who hides among the tombs since the last century, have been frequently sighted, especially at night when they seem to make direct contact and even converse with visitors. You may also encounter the Lady in White, a woman who wanders inconsolably among the graves, searching for her lost fiancé. Another woman, beautiful and blonde, is said to ask for a ride out of the cemetery, mysteriously disappearing along the way.

Poltergeist in Piauí

What appears to be the simple home of a kind grandmother on Rua Tiradentes in Piauí was actually the scene of a phenomenon incomprehensible to science. According to local residents, the small house was completely destroyed by spirits. Furniture would fly uncontrollably around the house, in a phenomenon known as poltergeist, where objects move under supernatural influence, seemingly weightless. The term "poltergeist" comes from German and means "noisy spirit," often associated with specific entities such as children or adolescents. In addition to moving objects, the phenomenon may involve inexplicable noises, flickering lights, and even touches, creating a scene worthy of a horror movie like The Conjuring.

Varginha, MG

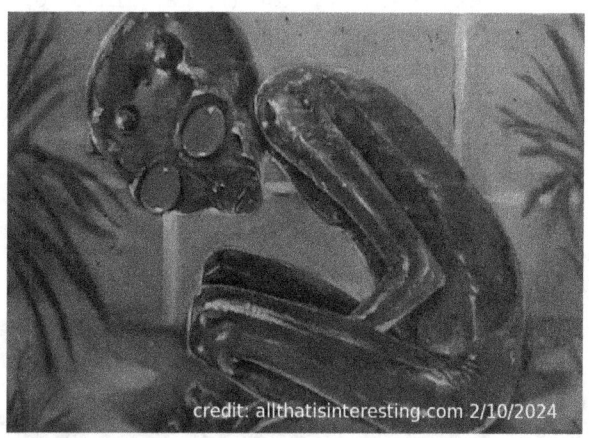

In 1996, in Varginha, in southern Minas Gerais, three girls claimed to have seen in a vacant lot, leaning against a wall, an extremely short creature with brown, viscous skin like that of a snake, three horn-like protuberances on its head, red eyes, and a foul odor. They told their parents in distress that they had seen the devil. Three animals died of unknown causes in the following months.

There were then numerous reports of sightings,

including one from a farmer and his wife, who claimed to have clearly seen a craft near the pasture that resembled a submarine. It is said that local authorities, the police, and the army were involved in the sightings and captured the exotic creature with a net.

Some residents claim that the government silenced the case, sending the creature for studies within the army, suppressing local media, and denying everything that was seen. However, later in a documentary, the army alleged that the creature was a homeless man, contradictorily claiming at another time that they had actually confused it with a couple of people with dwarfism who were in the hospital. The inconsistencies in the reports raised suspicions, with some even asserting that NASA was involved in the case.

The police officer who supposedly captured the alien died unexpectedly from a generalized infection, supposedly due to his contact with the creature, according to what the victim's family believes. Even today, Varginha remains one of the biggest hotspots for UFO researchers and enthusiasts worldwide, with various sculptures and establishments referencing the unusual phenomenon.

Haunted Mansion of Araraquara

credit: Casarão Bela Vista — Foto: Fabio Rodrigues/G1

In Araraquara, a city in the interior of São Paulo, there is a vast mansion that belonged to the family of a sadistic colonel, surrounded by coffee plantations, where extreme torture was inflicted on enslaved people during the colonial period. Torture, flogging, and punitive executions were common in his estate.

Visitors suggest that at certain times, one can hear the sound of chains being dragged across the floor, screams, and the passing of a carriage, accompanied by the sound of horse hooves trotting. Additionally, there are sudden drops in temperature, objects moving, and a constant feeling of oppression and being watched.

Legend has it that at midnight, the souls of enslaved individuals who managed to escape the colonel's rule freely roam the village. Another legend states that a great treasure of gold coins belonging to the colonel is hidden there, protected by a ghost. Several attempts to uncover the treasure have been made, but nothing has been found so far.

Martinelli Building

Although the Martinelli Building in São Paulo is now a notable tourist attraction, it has been the scene of several brutal crimes. For many years, it was the tallest building in Brazil, originally planned as a luxury residence for the elite.

It is said that before the building's foundation, the area and its surroundings were governed by the presence of Anhangá, an indigenous deity that was demonized after colonization and portrayed as the Devil. Anhangá was believed to cause illusions in people, leading them to flee reality and commit atrocities.

Years after the building's completion, a man was brutally murdered by strangulation and thrown into the elevator shaft. Subsequently, a teenage girl was killed by a man and thrown from the top of the building, her body discovered with lacerations and signs of torture. Additionally, drug trafficking, prostitution, suicides, and other unsolved murders occurred within the vast skyscraper, which transitioned from being a meeting place for São Paulo's nobility to becoming a slum.

Many visitors report hearing the sounds of people working, even when the building is empty, as well as feeling presences and an unusual pressure in their heads. The ghosts of the unsolved crimes haunt the visitors, unable to rest in peace without justice. Employees have even reported avoiding the building at night, claiming to see a blonde woman who slams doors, laughs, and disintegrates into thin air like a hologram.

Serra do Roncador

In the heart of Mato Grosso lies a mountain known as Serra do Roncador. This location is famous for mysterious lights, reports of dimensional portals, and occasional encounters with extraterrestrials. According to local legends, the mountain conceals a portal to Ratanabá, a lost city reminiscent of Atlantis.

The tale includes a British explorer named Colonel Percy Fawcett, who ventured to the mountain in search of a lost city he referred to as "Z." He is said to have disappeared in the jungle, possibly as a victim of inexplicable forces that protect the site. Today, it remains an important place for indigenous worship of nature's elements and is a destination for those seeking a "spiritual awakening."

Dear reader, would you have the courage to visit any of these places? If you ever come to Brazil, now you know where to avoid, unless you want nightmares and chills down your spine.

Puzzled by Sonali Roy

ARTICLE

Permutations of *The Picture of Dorian Gray*
Denise Noe

Governor Robinson, in his summation for Lizzie Borden's defense, said, "To find [Lizzie Borden] guilty you must believe she is a fiend. Does she look it?"

Anyone who has seen photographs of Lizzie Borden knows that the men of that jury did not see a great beauty when they looked at the defendant. Neither did they see someone horribly ugly. At 32, Lizzie Borden was a slightly plump woman with wide-set eyes and a softly tilting nose. She had light brown hair that she wore up in a loose bun in the fashion of the day.

At least one modern observer has found her appearance somewhat unsettling. In an article appearing in *Newsweek*, Florence Brigham, who was curator of the Fall River Historical Society for many years and whose mother-in-law testified as a character witness at the trial, was quoting as saying, "I always thought her eyes looked peculiar."

The "peculiar," rather pale appearance of Lizzie's eyes may have been the effect of the photography of the day. However, in his inquest testimony, Eli Bence, who claimed Lizzie had been in his drugstore the day prior to the murders attempting to buy a poison, described her as having "a peculiar expression around the eyes."

Despite the perceptions of both Bence and Brigham, a commentator who saw her in the flesh found her appearance utterly inconsistent with the heinous acts of which she was accused. Journalist Julian Ralph wrote, "She is no Medusa or Gorgon. There is nothing wicked, criminal, or hard in her features."

The expectation that an evil person should have distorted features reflecting inner depravity may be an irrational prejudice but it is certainly a common one. Perhaps it is human nature to expect, even against all logic, to see the inner life written on the outer visage,

That expectation, or rather the frustration of it, was

developed in a fascinating manner in Oscar Wilde's magnificent horror classic, *The Picture of Dorian Gray*. Published in 1891, just one year before the Borden murders, the novel opens in a painter's well-furnished studio, one filled with the rich and pleasant fragrance of fresh flowers. The mood is one of indolence and luxury as the reader meets friends Lord Henry Wotton and painter Basil Hallward. Basil has just painted a picture of a particularly handsome young man. The man is described as possessing ivory skin, cleanly delineated features with a curvy red mouth, and a head of golden curls. Both the painting itself and the attractive appearance of its subject strongly impress Lord Henry.

Basil informs Henry that the visage he so admires is that of Dorian Gray and soon introduces the aristocrat to Dorian. Henry idly remarks on how the beauty of Dorian will inevitably fade in time, with his face getting wrinkled and flabby, while the picture retains the freshness and glamour of his youth. A distressed Dorian expresses aloud the wish that it could be the other way around.

Lord Henry and Dorian become fast friends, or more accurately, mentor and pupil as the former fills the latter with the precepts of hedonism and the joys of a cynical, exploitative approach to other people.

Dorian soon finds himself enamored of a lovely young actress. Her name is Sybil Vane and she ardently returns his love and wants to marry him. She works in a low-rate theater but her talents shine despite the deficiencies of her co-workers. The naturalness with which she inhabits a variety of characters, bringing them to life on the stage with her utterly plausible simulation of their personalities and emotions has enthralled Dorian. He considers her a true genius among thespians and shares his idolization of her with Lord Henry and Basil. They are eager to see this brilliant actress in her glory and accompany Dorian to one of her performances. She is appearing as the female lead in *Romeo and Juliet*. Dorian can hardly wait to see this wondrously talented woman, beloved and in love, play the part of what may be the greatest love heroine ever created. He anticipates seeing Sybil as an enthralling Juliet.

At the theater, Dorian finds himself dismayed and disappointed. Sybil is as lovely as ever but her performance as Juliet is flat, forced, and artificial. Her acting is unnatural and uninspired. Her recital of her lines is listless and stilted. Dorian is crushed by this display of simple bad acting.

Afterwards, a disillusioned and heartsick Dorian goes backstage to confront her. He is amazed to find her seeming almost proud of her wretched performance. Smiling and happy, she proclaims, "How badly I acted tonight, Dorian!"

He readily agrees and asks if she is sick. No, she replies. She is not sick. She is in love, really in love, and so can no longer fake love. Reality has replaced, and displaced, art for her. Sybil tells him, "Dorian, before I knew you, acting was the one reality of my life. It was only in the theatre that I lived. I thought it was all true. . . .The painted scenes were my world. I knew nothing but shadows, and I thought them real. You came – oh, my beautiful love! – and you freed my soul from prison. You taught me what reality really is. Tonight, for the first time in my life, I saw through the hollowness, the sham, the silliness of the empty pageant in which I had always played. Tonight, for the first time, I became conscious that the Romeo was hideous, and old, and painted, that the moonlight in the orchard was false, that the scenery was vulgar, and that the words I had to speak were unreal, were not my words, were not what I wanted to say. You had brought me something higher, something of which all art is but reflection. You made me understand what love really is." That understanding, she indicated, took away the power of artifice necessary for her art.

Dorian was aghast. He fell in love with Sybil because of her talent as an actress. "You have killed my love," he tells her. He continues that he will never see her again or even think of her for without her art Sybil is "nothing."

Terrified and heartbroken, Sybil begs Dorian not to leave her. He and her love for him are her only reality. Dorian coldly spurns her. She pleads with him to give her another chance. She promises to try to regain her acting powers and reminds him that she only gave a disappointing performance one time.

Dorian is unmoved and tells her that this is goodbye, leaving her crushed.

When Dorian returns home, he happens to take a look at his portrait. He is astonished by what he sees. There appears to be a subtle but definite alteration in the painting as there is "a touch of cruelty in the mouth." Dorian tells himself he must be imagining things. Again and again he checks the portrait. Each time he sees that slight change, that "cruelty in the mouth."

This leads him to some soul-searching that begins that evening and continues through the next afternoon. He concludes that, however "monstrous" it seems, the wish he had made when the painting was first finished had somehow been granted. Then he determines to turn this odd, supernatural fortune to good use. He decides that the painting will "be to him the visible emblem of conscience." He will resist temptation and conduct himself with moral rectitude to prevent further troubling alterations to the portrait. No longer will he follow Lord Henry's cynical, hedonistic theories.

He also realizes that the "cruelty in the mouth" reflects the truth of his treatment of Sybil Vane and he resolves to set matters right. Despite his disappointment over her performance, he will marry her. The next day, he writes a long letter to Sybil telling her that he was sorry for his mistreatment of her and asking her forgiveness. A sense of being clean and whole fills him when he finishes this epistle.

Lord Henry pays a call. He is distressed and wishes to comfort Dorian. "Do you mean about Sybil Vane?" Dorian queries and receives the reply, "Yes, of course."

Dorian does not appear to need much comforting for which Lord Henry is glad – until he learns that the reason for Dorian's good spirits is that he plans to marry Sybil Vane. Lord Henry informs him that Sybil is dead, an apparent suicide.

Shocked, Dorian also realizes he is not as devastated by this news as many men would be and wonders if it reflects a lack of normal feeling. He is calmed by Lord Henry's reassurances and spends the evening at the Opera.

It is quite possible that Oscar Wilde intended Sybil's Vane's last name to be heavily and doubly symbolic. It may represent both her own vanity that could not survive a loved one's rejection and Dorian's, which led him both to that rejection and to a shallow, self-absorbed reaction to her death. It is also likely that it has the connotations of a weathervane since Dorian's relationship with her, a relationship fatal for her, is a portent of the direction his life will take.

Dorian has accepted the supernatural reality that his portrait will take on both the signs of his aging and those of his debaucheries and cruelties. He moves the portrait into the attic to keep it hidden from other eyes.

At this critical juncture in Dorian's life, Lord Henry leaves him a book. Wilde never names that book but tells us that Dorian found it "the strangest book that he had ever read." Wilde goes on to describe it as "a psychological study of a certain young Parisian, who spent his life trying to realize in the nineteenth century all the passions and modes of thought that belonged to every century except his own." Wilde continues that it was "a poisonous book" that endlessly fascinated Dorian.

Sources this writer has consulted indicate that the "poisonous book" was almost certainly *A Rebours* a novel by Karl Huysman that was first published in 1884.

This book, coupled with the seductive cynicisms of Lord Henry, leads Dorian to discard the initial decision to use his portrait as a kind of visual conscience and guide to good behavior. Dorian adopts a hedonistic lifestyle and ruthless, exploitive stance toward others.

Wilde leaves the exact nature of Dorian's wrongs vague. The reader is told, "Even those who had heard the most evil things against him, and from time to time strange rumours about his mode of life crept through London and became the chatter of the clubs, could not believe anything to his dishonor when they saw him. He had always the look of one who had kept himself unspotted from the world." Wilde writes that Dorian frequently took "mysterious and prolonged absences that gave rise to such strange conjecture among those who were his friends" and spent time in the "sordid room of the little ill-famed tavern near the Docks . . ."

Soon after these passages, Wilde makes clear the sexual nature of some of Dorian's transgressions: "Women who had wildly adored him, and for his sake had braved all social censure and set convention at defiance, were seen to grow pallid with shame or horror if Dorian Gray entered the room."

Basil Hallward confronts Dorian about his increasingly blighted reputation, quoting an acquaintance as saying, "you were a man whom no pure-minded girl should be allowed to know, and whom no chaste woman should sit in the same room with." That is enough to let the reader know that Dorian is an experienced and wily seducer, that he may have sired out-of-wedlock pregnancies and impregnated married women.

The painter continues, "Why is your friendship so fatal to young men?' He runs through a list of Dorian's male friends, one of whom committed suicide, another of whom fled England to escape the disgrace of a sullied reputation, and others who found themselves ostracized and ruined.

Dorian then talks about how one man married an unsuitable woman and another forged a friend's name on a check and says he can hardly be held responsible for his friends' bad choices or their "vices" and "debaucheries."

Part of the reason for the vagueness of terms and allusions is that Wilde could not in the book baldly state one of the major "vices" Dorian was practicing, that of homosexual relations. It was Wilde's own lover, Lord Alfred Douglas, who coined the term "the love that dare not speak its name" for eroticism between men.

Thinly veiled references to gay male preferences and behavior permeate *The Picture of Dorian Gray*. Dorian's very name probably comes from that of an ancient Greek tribe called the Dorians and characters frequently make references to ancient Greece.

Oscar Wilde once said that having homosexual

relations in his Victorian culture was so dangerous that it was like "feasting with panthers." It is natural that he would be fascinated by ancient Hellenic culture in which sexual love between men was accepted and even glorified.

While it is significant that there are so many references to male homosexuality in the novel, it is wrong to say the book is simply "about" homosexuality. There is a danger of underestimating the work of artists if we see their works solely in terms of sexuality, and this danger is especially pronounced in the case of both gay male and lesbian artists.

Wilde himself has been variously described as bisexual or homosexual. The Dorian Gray described the novel is flamboyantly bisexual, a man who seduces both women and men with equal abandon although the same-sex side of his sexual equation can never be explicitly named.

Like Oscar Wilde and the unforgettable character of Dorian Gray that he created, the sexuality – or lack thereof – of Lizzie Borden has been the subject of much conjecture. Lizzie never married. Some commentators such as Ann Jones, author of *Women Who Kill*, believe that the trip she took to Europe prior to the murders was a husband-hunting trip that netted no husband. The famous Trickey-McHenry Affair had a newspaper publishing the story that the 32-year-old Lizzie was "in trouble" at the time of the murders, a story that turned out to be made up out of whole cloth as she was not pregnant and had no reason to fear she was.

Suitors hover in the background of many Borden theories with Lizzie wanting a man but unable to marry him because of Andrew's opposition. Some stories that hold Lizzie was guilty suggest she murdered because he was incestuously abusing her while more Freudian versions postulate that she killed out of a taboo yen for her father.

There is no solid evidence that Lizzie ever had a suitor or wanted one. It is quite possible that she was simply without romantic or sexual yearnings. A recent study found that 1-3% of the population is asexual. The percentage who at least thought of themselves in this way had to be larger in the repressed Victorian era, especially among women.

It is also possible that Lizzie was a (perhaps unconscious) lesbian. There were rumors to this effect during her lifetime. Agnes DeMille published the story in *Lizzie Borden, Dance of Death* that a man divorcing his wife on grounds of lesbianism had named her as co-respondent but that the judge dismissed the case as "frivolous." Leonard Rebello has written that there is no known record of any such lawsuit

Years after her acquittal, Lizzie had an intense friendship with the lovely actress Nance O'Neil. There were rumors at the time that their relationship was a romance and many writers have believed that the pair enjoyed a love affair.

It is quite possible that they did. However, conjecture is not proof. We must also remember that unacceptable sexual feelings are often repressed and that those who have them may not even be conscious of them. This is especially true of women who may be more likely to think of themselves simply as especially "pure" if they have little or no attraction to men. Their relationships with other women may be sexual without the parties ever being aware of it.

Indeed, one difference between male and female homosexuality may be that it is far easier for women to even *participate* in sexual activities without knowing that they are doing so. Women who consider themselves traditionally "chaste" may sleep in the same bed, hug each other as friends, and eventually start rubbing a bit until they discover that this can lead to a very good feeling indeed. However, if they are sexual innocents who have never even heard the word "orgasm" and associate sexuality with men, they are unlikely to put the same construction that a more sophisticated person would on their private discoveries.

The Victorian era was especially apt to be a time when lesbian feelings were misunderstood or unacknowledged. While male homosexuality was the love that dare not speak its name, female homosexuality was often the love that did not know it. After all, in the same England that put Oscar Wilde in prison for private consensual homosexual activities, no woman could be prosecuted for lesbianism. It had been included in the original version of the bill on penalties for homosexuality but Queen Victoria refused to sign the bill until all references to women were removed. Lesbianism did not exist, she declared, and she would not sign anything that impugned the honorable tradition of women's love.

The situation regarding lesbian invisibility may have been slightly different in the United States but it is a certainty that its existence was something unspoken in polite company and often unacknowledged even by women whose true yearnings were in that direction.

However, the truth that the character of Lizzie's sexuality is the subject of much conjecture and that there is some reason to believe that, if she were sexual at all, her sexuality included an attraction to members of her own gender, gives her something in common with both Oscar Wilde and his fictional creation of Dorian Gray. There is a Greek connection as well since "Sapphic love" as a term for women's erotic love comes from the Greek poet Sappho.

The Picture of Dorian Gray has been made into a movie several times. The most famous, and possibly the best, cinematic treatment of it is the 1945 version directed by Albert Lewin who also wrote its screenplay. Hurd Hatfield stars as Dorian Gray, George Sanders plays Lord Henry Wotton, Lowell Gilmore plays Basil Hallward, and Angela Lansbury plays Sybil Vance.

While sticking fairly close to its origins, the movie makes significant departures from Wilde's novel. One change is that the movie places a statue of a black cat, said to have been sculpted in ancient Egypt and to represent a feline god, near Dorian when he makes his fervent wish that the picture would grow old while he remains young. Thus, there is a horror-movie "explanation" for the granting of Dorian's wish. This clever addition lends the tale an extra bit of spookiness.

Interestingly, just as the ancient Greek and ancient Roman cultures have an association with male homosexuality, ancient Egypt has an association with the eerie. The link between ancient Egypt and the supernatural is undoubtedly because no other culture put so much work into a hoped-for afterlife with its practice of mummification and its tombs built as pyramids.

Another alteration the movie makes is in the depiction of Dorian. The character in Wilde's novel is described as having a cherub-like appearance with a head of golden curls and is often emotionally expressive. Hurd Hatfield has dark, slicked-back hair and plays Dorian with an almost complete lack of affect. Like the black cat-god, this absence of expression works to intensify the sense of horror.

One extremely significant way in which the movie differs from its source is in the reason why Dorian breaks his engagement to Sibyl Vane, a theatrical singer in this film. Lord Henry tells him to test her chastity by giving her an ultimatum, threatening to end their relationship unless she agrees to a premarital sexual relationship. If Dorian successfully seduces her, he should make the break permanent. While one *Internet Movie Database* reviewer found Lansbury's performance "a little too demure for a theatrical singer from the East End," that demure appearance was necessary to convey the idea of her sexual innocence. That innocence makes her succumbing to Dorian seem all the more painful for her.

The change of the source of Dorian's disillusionment from Sybil's unexpected failure as an actress to his successful seduction of her works to obscure one of the primary theme's of the story, the uneasy relationship between art and reality. However, the expression of this theme through contrastingly good and poor acting performances might have been difficult to translate from prose to the silver screen.

Overall, the 1945 cinematic *The Picture of Dorian Gray* is a wonderfully entertaining and exquisitely rendered motion picture. It is filmed in black and white except for the showings of Dorian's portrait that switch suddenly to a lush color. George Sanders plays the part of Lord Henry in the oily and glib manner that he has used successfully in his many world-weary roles.

Oscar Wilde's *The Picture of Dorian Gray* is a novel that shows off the full range of its author's brilliance. As might be expected in a book by a man who could easily be considered the King of the One-Liners, it is rich in witticisms and arresting descriptions. Lord Henry says, "The one charm of marriage is that it makes a life of deception absolutely necessary for both parties." The reader is told that a character is "a perfect saint amongst women, but so dreadfully dowdy that she reminded one of a badly bound hymn-book."

It is important not to mistake Wilde's wit for shallowness, as there is often great depth within his epigrams that can point out major paradoxes in many areas of life. *The Picture of Dorian Gray* is about many things including the relationship between art and life, between images and truth, and the nature of temptation, of good and evil, and of identity, It is also about sexuality. Perhaps above all, it is an enthralling, eerie, and beautifully told story.

This classic fiction has some parallels already noted to the Lizzie Borden mystery. The ultimate link may be that both fictional story and real-life mystery are inextricably linked to the Victorian era yet both continue to fascinate across time and cultural divides.

Sources

The Picture of Dorian Gray by Oscar Wilde.
Trial of Lizzie Andrew Borden, 2001 copyright Harry Widdows for LizzieAndrewBorden.com.
"A New Whack at the Borden Case," *Newsweek*, June 4, 1984.
Ceremonies of the Heart, edited by Becky Butler.
Lizzie Borden, Dance of Death by Agnes DeMille.
Women Who Kill by Ann Jones.
Lizzie Borden Past & Present by Leonard Rebello.
Internet Movie Database.

"The Artist's Studio," http://www.nyu.edu/library/bobst/research/fales/exhibits/wilde/5studio.htm.

www.ingramcontent.com/pod-product-compliance
Lightning Source LLC
LaVergne TN
LVHW012021060526
838201LV00061B/4399